Could Be Something Good

Timber Falls, Volume 1

Fiona West

Published by Tempest and Kite, 2020.

This is a work of fiction. Similarities to real people, places, or events are entirely coincidental.

COULD BE SOMETHING GOOD

First edition. May 29, 2020.

ISBN: 978-1-952172-02-1

Written by Fiona West.

CHAPTER ONE

"A LITTLE TO THE LEFT." Ainsley gestured over with her hand.

Sweat dripping down his light skin, Daniel shuffled forward slightly as his dark-haired brother mirrored his movements, stepping backward.

"Hmm. Is that too far?" The petite blonde tapped her fair chin, standing in the middle of her apartment's living room. "Can you move it back to the right?"

"Take your time, Slick, it's not like this is heavy or anything," Daniel quipped, grinning, adjusting his hold on the modern gray IKEA couch.

"You're being compensated, aren't you?" Ainsley said, crossing her arms.

Daniel shook his head at her. "Buchanan, these hands are made to treat patients, not move furniture." He paused when her gaze dropped to the floor. "Of course, your baked goods more than make up for it."

She sighed and threw up her hands. "Okay, good enough. Come get your pay."

He made eye contact with his brother Kyle, and they both gently set down their sides in unison. Despite being brothers, they didn't look much alike: both were about the same height (six foot one), but the resemblance ended there. Kyle took after their father with his dark hair and brown eyes, while Daniel's dirty blond hair and blue eyes looked more like their mother's. Kyle's hair was short, messy, but he did nothing to fix it. Daniel's longer style was sliding out of the high top knot he'd put it in last night, and he took a moment to fix it before he followed them into the kitchen. Kyle, still wearing the suit he'd worn to the hospital, had already polished off his first brownie. Daniel shook his head in mock astonishment when he caught his brother watching Ainsley bend over to get the milk from the fridge. Kyle's narrowed eyes told him he was not happy to be caught staring, and Daniel chuckled. They both fixed their faces into a placid neutral as she turned back to them.

"I really appreciate this, you guys," she said, as she tipped the milk carton. "Did I mention that? I appreciate you."

"What are best friends for?" Daniel asked, bumping her shoulder with his. "I'm here for you. And Kyle's here for brownies."

His brother lifted one dark eyebrow as he reached for another treat. "I'm here for her, too. I just know a good thing when I see it." Ainsley and Daniel both grinned at him.

"So you're getting a new roommate, huh?"

She nodded, gesturing to the living room with her glass. "Just wanted to move things around in case she has furniture."

"Is she new in town?"

"I think so? I don't know." Ainsley pulled out a package of chicken thighs and piled red peppers and sweet onions on the counter.

"Didn't you interview her?" Kyle asked, and Daniel heard the discontented edge in his voice.

"Now, now, Grumpy," Daniel said, grabbing another brownie, "Ainsley's an adult. She wouldn't cohabitate with anyone who'd harm her, I'm sure. And if she does, we likely won't know until it's too late, anyway."

"It's Timber Falls," she said, rolling her eyes. "What's going to happen? Is she going to drown me in the Santiam River? Bury me in the national forest, never to be heard from again?"

"A lot could happen," Kyle insisted.

"Kyle, the only town more boring than this is actually named Boring."

"What does she do, your roommate?" Daniel asked through a giant bite. "Does she work in town?"

"She's a doula, I think. Or a midwife, maybe? Can't remember. Some kind of caretaking profession." She turned to Kyle. "See? Very safe."

"Or she has access to the medications to kill you in your sleep," Kyle muttered, but only Daniel heard him; Ainsley was too busy searching her cupboards for a package of corn tortillas.

"We should probably get going," Daniel said, wiping the crumbs off his hands and shirt, glancing with masked amusement at his brother. He didn't say the rest of what he was thinking: *We should probably get going before Kyle starts audibly growling at the idea of someone living with Ainsley who isn't him.*

"Oh," she said, her face falling, "I thought you were staying for fajitas? We have to celebrate your new residency thing!"

"Kyle's got important brooding to do, I think."

"Can't you just stay for dinner?" she pleaded. "I'm trying out a new recipe and I need guinea pigs. Please?"

Kyle met Ainsley's gaze briefly, then looked away. "You got any beer?"

Five fajitas, a Sprite, two more brownies, and a rom com later, Daniel headed down the stairs of Ainsley's apartment, rubbing his overfull belly with regret. Somehow, he'd ended up on the couch in the middle between his rather agitated older brother and his very oblivious best friend.

Daniel grinned at him. "You wanna talk about Ainsley?"

Kyle's face gave away nothing. "Nope."

"Okay. But I hear that too much pining can give you hives."

"You're the worst doctor in the world."

"Just because you're not a resident anymore doesn't mean you know everything, Dr. Durand. Severe emotional stress can be a trigger."

"I'm not distressed. There's nothing to feel distressed about."

"That's funny," Daniel said, as he unlocked his Volvo and slid inside, "because you seemed pretty distressed about her living with an unapproved roommate."

"It's just a stupid thing to do," he griped. "You've got to vet people."

Daniel nodded, starting the car. "But you know Ainsley. She's better at getting in over her head than all the city kids falling into Detroit Lake every summer."

Kyle grunted in what Daniel assumed was agreement.

"If it'll make you feel better, I'll stop by and meet the roommate next week." Daniel kept all hints of teasing out of his voice.

"It's not about how I feel; it's about her not letting a serial killer move into her second bedroom." Kyle paused. "And get some references from the woman, for God's sake."

"I feel like Ainsley might take issue with you calling her roommate's references . . ."

"I'm not going to *call them*, I'm just going to internet stalk them to see what kind of people they are."

"Kyle." His brother turned to look at him. "Just ask her out already."

He turned back to the window. "She doesn't see me that way."

Daniel wasn't so convinced; she never made an effort to hang out with Kyle one-on-one, but she often suggested that Daniel bring him along. As far as he knew, she didn't date because she was "too busy." The busyness was largely of her own making, since she was on almost every committee in town that it was possible to join. If something was cooking around Timber Falls, Ainsley had her spoon in it.

Kyle had been "secretly" pining for her for about eight years now. It was the worst-kept secret in the Durand family, and no one could figure out why he never did anything about it. Their oldest brother, Philip, had asked him once and been met with grunting and several days of stony silence, so they'd mostly left him alone about it.

Since Kyle had descended into thoughtful silence, Daniel did a little thinking of his own. He loved Ainsley—of course he did. But the idea of dating her was laughable. They were far too alike. And he enjoyed spending time with her, obviously, but he wondered if he wasn't leaning on her friendship a little too heavily for female companionship. He'd gone on lots of casual dates, had some casual hook-ups, but hadn't had an actual girlfriend in years. There were lots of reasons for this, of course; there was always a reason when you were in medical school. Even his undergrad had been tough academically—though the amount of time he spent biking and reading comic books probably hadn't helped his studies. But he would do something about that, the dating thing. Just as soon as he figured out who to ask.

He glanced over at Kyle, who was still ignoring him completely. It was too easy to mess with him; if he had feathers, they'd be constantly ruffled where Ainsley was concerned.

"Well, if you're not going to ask her out," Daniel drawled, "maybe I should."

Kyle snorted. "Ha."

"Ha? What 'ha'?"

"She'd never go out with you."

Daniel pulled into the driveway of the two-story white farmhouse they shared. "How can you be so sure?"

"Go ahead. Ask her." They both sat there as he texted. His phone swooshed.

"Well?"

Daniel cleared his throat. "She replied with a gif of a baby falling over laughing. Then she asked if I'd been kidnapped and this was some kind of signal that I needed help."

Kyle grinned, then got out of the car and sauntered inside, whistling.

CHAPTER TWO

DANIEL WAS AT THE HOSPITAL early on Friday; he had first-week jitters and didn't want to chance being late. He loitered outside the conference room where his residency group was meeting, having already finished checking his patients. Dr. Udawatte and Dr. Trout seemed nice. It was just the three of them; rural residency programs were always smaller, so that's what he'd expected. Less funding available than for the big programs, even though the need for doctors was greater here than in the big metropolitan areas. He watched people moving around with the kind of paced intentionality he thought medical professionals possessed in greater measure than most people. Well, maybe not counting moms of small children. They seemed to know it was a marathon. If only doctors could wear yoga pants all day, too.

"Excuse me." A tall blonde woman swept past him shouldering an oversized canvas bag that was stuffed to the brim, talking with a dark-haired woman next to her. Her hair was damp, and the scent of lavender lingered in the air behind her. Daniel Durand was too sensible to believe in love at first sight . . . but there was something about this woman. He couldn't begin to put his finger on it. Her no-nonsense gait? Her curvy hips? The slight gravelly quality to her voice?

Daniel suddenly knew he had a soul for the first time, and its first order of business was declaring that it had found its mate. The pull toward her was planetary: he felt like a meteor drawn to her by an immense gravity the likes of which he'd never felt before. She'd only said two words to him, but he had butterflies in his belly like they'd just stayed up all night talking. He felt itchy to somehow do just that; he wanted to talk to her so badly, he felt it like a hunger, like he hadn't eaten in days. And God help him if she smiled at him.

The woman and her friend paused near the elevators, and Daniel caught sight of his brother and waved him over.

"Who is that?"

"Who?"

"The blonde."

Kyle squinted down the hall. "Oh. That's Winnie. She's a midwife."

"Why haven't I seen her before?"

"I don't know," he said slowly, "do you need glasses?"

Daniel rolled his eyes. "I *have* glasses, as you already know."

"Have you ever thought about laser . . ."

Daniel walked away while Kyle was still talking.

"Hi," he said, interrupting the other nurse she was talking to. "I'm Dr. Durand."

Her eyebrows made a deep V. "No, you're not. I've met Dr. Durand. Twice."

"I'm the older one's son and the younger one's brother, Daniel Durand. The other Dr. Durand," he said, smiling. He offered his hand, but she didn't take it.

She did not seem amused. "Well, Other Dr. Durand, you're interrupting my conversation with Nurse Lopez." She turned back to her colleague.

Rebuffed? Was he being rebuffed? Strange. And troubling . . . very troubling. He walked slowly back to where Kyle was watching him with silent amusement.

"You need water or something to put out those flames?"

He frowned, rubbing the back of his neck. "She said I was interrupting."

"Yeah, she's not interested in you, man. You're gonna have to change up your moves if you want Winnie Baker to like you."

"Baker? As in, related to Dr. Baker? My attending physician?" *That's not good.*

He nodded. "Her mother."

"I'm not sure 'mother' could really apply to Dr. Baker," Daniel said, lowering his voice. "I mean, 'mother' conjures up images of warm blankets and freshly baked treats and lunch box love notes."

"That doesn't seem like her thing."

"Whose thing?" Both brothers jumped.

I should've known better, thought Daniel, turning to face their father.

"What are you doing here?" Kyle asked; he always recovered a little faster.

"Just checking on my boys." Evan Durand grinned. "I was in the neighborhood."

"Snooping, you mean," said Daniel, nudging him with his shoulder. He could see in his peripheral vision that Drs. Udawatte and Trout had just entered a patient's room. "I should get back to my group." He left them chatting in the hall, glad that his dad hadn't witnessed his apparently foolish intention to introduce himself to the lavender woman. Perhaps it was only foolish because he'd jumped in too quickly, as usual. A little reconnaissance first . . . maybe that's what the situation called for. Then again, his attending's daughter? Was that a good idea?

It had taken a year longer than he'd wanted to get back to Timber Falls—he'd been at OHSU in Portland the year before for his first year of residency. But thanks to his dad pulling some strings, he'd gotten Santiam for his second year of residency. There was a huge need for rural physicians, so this new rural residency program was a great way to give doctors a taste of the job, as well as open up more postings. Santiam had gotten a grant just a few years ago.

He'd narrowed his focus to family medicine his first year and was enjoying the opportunity to see patients of all ages, but he liked kids especially; pediatrics was a little less intense than cardiac and emergency, a little more intense than podiatry and dermatology. Then again, doctors had to manage both patient and parent when working with kids.

He joined Udawatte and Trout in Mr. Helsing's room. To his surprise, of his current patients, he looked forward to seeing Mr. Helsing a little more than the others, even though Kyle and his dad both told him that he shouldn't have favorites. For one thing, he was seventy-four, but he didn't let that keep him from hitting on all the nurses—respectfully, of course. It was how Daniel secretly imagined himself as an old man. You couldn't walk out of Perry Helsing's room without laughing, and Daniel respected that the man could keep a sense of humor while facing bronchitis. He'd be going home soon, and Daniel was going to miss him.

His attending physician, Dr. Baker, walked in, her cool gaze surveying her interns, then straightened her black pencil skirt under her white coat. Now that he knew they were related, he could see the strong resemblance between Dr. Baker and her daughter, the soulmate who'd just given him the brush-off.

"Mr. Helsing," Dr. Baker greeted him, businesslike as usual.

"Good morning, Dr. Baker, you're looking lovely today. What's the prognosis?" He winked at Dr. Udawatte. "Heard that on *Diagnosis Murder* once."

Tharushi grinned at him, but sobered when Dr. Baker placed the diaphragm of her stethoscope against his chest and listened to his lungs. She motioned for all of them to do the same. Daniel was last in line.

"The prognosis is good," Dr. Baker replied. "Your chest X-rays came back clean. We're going to start you on another dose of antibiotics, just to be sure." She turned to leave and the other two followed her.

"Well, with four doctors instead of one, it was bound to be good." Mr. Helsing dropped his voice so only Daniel could hear. "Hey, send that nurse in here, will you?"

"Which nurse?" Daniel asked, mimicking the man's hushed tone.

"The blonde one, the big girl. The baby catcher."

Everyone else had shuffled back toward the door, and he lengthened his steps to catch up with them.

"If I figure out which one that is, I'll do that."

"Tell her I'm short on Vitamin U."

Daniel grinned and shut the door quietly. Apparently, he wasn't the only one who wanted to talk to Winnie.

CHAPTER THREE

"I DON'T UNDERSTAND this, Winifred." Her mother sighed from her bedroom doorway. "You'll save a considerable amount of money if you continue to live here."

Winnie set her stack of neatly folded sweaters into a hard-sided blue suitcase, then bent to retrieve a pair of flip-flops that had fallen off the bed, but her hands groped fruitlessly under the pinstriped pink dust ruffle.

"You're only going to be here until the fall. What's the point of moving now, just to move again?"

There was no point in responding, thought Winnie. It wasn't really a conversation, just another lecture she was required to attend. Still, she tried to listen politely instead of rolling her eyes; it only made the lecture longer, and she considered herself too old for such teenage antics now that she was over thirty. Feeling for the shoes under her twin bed with no success, she finally knelt and lifted the dust ruffle to look. Dusty, but otherwise fine, her sandals sat between her MCAT study prep book and the flute case she hadn't touched since senior year of high school. *No reason to take either of those.*

"I'll be closer to the hospital."

"The drive is exactly the same," her mother replied, her silk blouse rustling as she crossed her arms.

"Yes, but it's a shorter distance. Better for the environment."

Her mother owned a Prius, which was ridiculous considering the likelihood of snow in the foothills of the Cascades, and Winnie hoped this last argument would distract her from asking again about her motivations for moving.

"How did you find this person again?"

Winnie stood up and folded a pair of leggings that had gotten mussed. "This person? Her name is Ainsley Buchanan, and she's an elementary school teacher. There was a post on the bulletin board at the library. I figure anyone who likes to read can't be too bad. From our phone conversations and emails, she sounds like someone I'd get along with."

"Well, you're always welcome here." *Translation: I think this is going to crash and burn like the* Hindenburg. Still, Winnie did appreciate her mother's willingness to back her up in the event that this was, in fact, a bad idea.

"Thanks, Mom." She gave her a kiss on the cheek as she went to get her shower stuff. "Do we have more boxes somewhere?"

Sandra Baker, unused to being defied, huffed her displeasure and went to the kitchen to brew herself another cup of coffee, Winnie assumed. *Whatever.* She was thirty-four now. She didn't have to listen to everything her mother said. Probably shouldn't, in fact. But Sandra Baker could be a force of nature when she wanted to be. It made her an excellent doctor.

When she'd finished packing mostly everything, she poked her head between the French doors of her mother's office. "Are you going to come meet Ainsley?"

"Perhaps another time," her mother said, not looking up from whatever she was typing on her computer. Winnie told herself for the hundredth time that there was no profit in feeling hurt by it.

"But we're still having dinner on Sunday?"

Her mother nodded. "Your grandparents are looking forward to it."

"Me too." She shifted her bag higher on her shoulder. "I guess I'll see you then unless we cross paths at work. Love you."

She did look up then. "I love you, too, sweetheart." Her mother got up from her desk and wrapped Winnie in a tight hug. "Be careful, okay?"

"Always am," she said, smiling.

"And you need a haircut."

"Got one scheduled for Tuesday if I don't get called in."

Based on her light scowl and previous comments, Winnie knew her mother loved routine too much to ever live by a nurse midwife's unpredictable schedule. That didn't matter much to Winnie. Not when she could help someone make their family bigger, share their love with a brand-new person. Make their baby's arrival into this world as peaceful and joyful and empowering as possible.

"Just make sure it gets done. Your ends are looking frayed."

Winnie touched her hair self-consciously, then with a sigh headed back up the stairs to grab the last of her boxes.

IT WAS SIX O'CLOCK by the time she'd finished unloading everything at the apartment. She trudged up the stairs with one last load, her quads burning from all the trips up and down and up and down. Thank God for Ainsley's cheerful insistence that she help, or she'd probably have another hour of work ahead of her. Instead, she could order a pizza for both of them, take a long shower, put sheets on the bed and start organizing her clothes—

"Knock knock." A genial male voice behind her made her jump.

Who just yells "knock knock" instead of, you know, knocking? *The door's already open.*

Ainsley's face lit. "Hey, you. Come on in. Winnie, this is my friend, Daniel."

A nervous shock to her stomach scattered her thoughts of how the evening might go. *No, it couldn't be . . .* She turned to see Daniel Durand, the obnoxious interrupter from the hospital. He was wearing another flirty grin, and Winnie glared at him before catching herself. Her new roommate was obviously friends with this man. She'd have to at least try to be civil to him.

She stuck out her hand. "We met at the hospital. I'm Winifred Baker."

"Well," he said slowly, "we didn't exactly meet, since you wouldn't even give me your name." He was still grinning, so it obviously hadn't bothered him too much. In fact, he seemed delighted by their interactions. How odd.

"I apologize," she said, smoothing her hair back. "I was in the middle of a conversation."

"And I probably should've waited until you were done. But when such a beautiful woman brushes by me, it's hard not to want to get her name and number immediately."

Winnie pinned him with a hard stare. "Does that work?"

His smile finally faltered. "Does what work?"

"That line."

"It's not a line, actually. It's just the truth." Now he was the one glaring; much to her surprise, his lips, framed by a neatly trimmed light beard, turned down. She couldn't help but notice how long his eyelashes were; it was kind of unfair for a man that handsome to have such pretty eyes, too. The hair on top of his head was longer, pulled back into a top knot, the sides undercut in a way she recognized was fashionable. That was a good word for him: *fashionable*. Dressed in trendy clothes with a hairstyle that required effort, but also the kind of guy who would throw you away the moment he got bored: fashionable. Winnie glanced at her new roommate, who looked truly curious about what was happening here.

"Well," Ainsley said, cutting through the tension, "I'm glad you've met now. Daniel, were you stopping by for a reason or just being friendly?"

His smile returned as his gaze fell on Ainsley. "Just being friendly, Slick. Unless you have brownies, in which case I'm here for a sugar hit." Winnie was having a hard time telling the exact nature of their relationship, but it was nothing she wanted to insert herself into. It appeared he would be around often, at any rate, and though she couldn't pretend to be excited about that, she didn't have to sulk over it.

Winnie started backing toward the hallway. "Well, I have a lot of unpacking to do . . ." It was the truth, after all.

He stepped forward, offering his hand. "Nice to meet you for real this time, Winifred Baker."

She glanced at Ainsley, who was trying to hide her reaction behind her fist: amusement. Pushing her shoulders back, Winnie took his hand and shook it firmly.

"You too, Dr. Durand."

"Other Dr. Durand," he corrected, grinning, releasing her hand, shoving his own deep into his dark-wash jeans pocket, like he didn't know what to do with it now.

She shot him a double thumbs up, then turned and hurried down the hallway. *What on earth was that?* She'd never done that gesture before in her life, and she stared down at her hands, as if demanding an explanation for their strange behavior. *Lashes. That's the explanation. His eyelashes.*

CHAPTER FOUR

DANIEL WAS STILL SCRATCHING his head when he arrived at his parents' house a few minutes later. The garage door was open, his father's touring bike still sitting out from a ride earlier, so he let himself in that way. He'd worked earlier, then gone home to shower before heading over to Ainsley's to check on the new roommate like he'd promised Kyle—and discovered to his delight that the beautiful woman who'd brushed him off, the woman who was his attending physician's daughter, was also his best friend's new roommate. His initial thought, that the universe was rewarding his boldness in approaching her early in the week, was quickly replaced with a conviction that it might not be a reward, at least not the quick and easy kind. He couldn't put his finger on exactly why he liked her; she was beautiful, of course, but she also obviously didn't tolerate fools. Unfortunately, she'd already classified him as a Grade-A Fool from the moment they met. Well, it was unfortunate, but it wasn't insurmountable.

"Knock knock," Daniel called as he opened the front door and let himself in, wiping his feet on the mat. The rain had just stopped for the first time all day. January was truly the longest month of the year.

Kyle looked up from the den where he was playing a game of Battleship with their nephew, Cooper. "Well?"

"Winifred Baker, the midwife. That's the new roommate."

Kyle looked at the ceiling like he was doing math in his head as he considered this. "That should be okay. She give you the cold shoulder again?"

"Sort of . . ." Daniel smoothed his hair back against his head. "But I think she'll warm up to me."

"Who will?" Cooper asked, looking between his uncles.

"It's your move," Kyle informed the boy. "Still."

"That's really nice of you to play Battleship, Uncle Kyle," Daniel said, using a tone that reminded him of Ainsley's teacher voice, as he strolled into the kitchen to find an appetizer.

"Wasn't my first choice," he grumbled. "It was either this or go for another bike ride with Dad, and I hated the first one. Go, Coop."

"B3."

"You already asked that one. Aren't you marking your misses?"

"My misses?" Cooper asked, perplexed. "Why would I mark my . . . oh. Um, can we start over?"

Daniel chuckled as he went into the kitchen. "Mom?"

"Just me," his sister replied, looking up from the book she was reading on her stool at the kitchen counter. He gave Maggie a kiss on the temple, then tugged on her wavy brown braid. It killed their mom that she put so little effort into her appearance, he knew; Daniel secretly admired Maggie for being true to herself.

"Just you, Eeyore?" he teased, and she rolled her eyes at him.

"Where've you been, anyway?" she asked, slipping a paper napkin on the counter into her book as a bookmark. "I've hardly seen you."

"I would think junior year would be keeping you plenty busy without your big brother around to entertain you, sis."

"Then you'd be wrong," she said, lifting her chin, and he chuckled so hard, his shoulders shook. He pulled her into a long hug, and she greedily squeezed him back; she'd always been a kid who craved touch. Seemed like his mom never put Maggie down her first two years of life. Even though he was almost ten years older than her, they'd always been the ones subjecting the rest of the family to their aggressive couch snuggling, much to Kyle's chagrin.

"Sorry, Mags, I've been really busy with my residency. I'll try to come around more." She'd never come to the hospital willingly, he knew. Childhood cancer had a way of making hospitals synonymous with hell.

"I forgive you. I guess."

"Canasta later?" he asked, popping an olive from a veggie tray into his mouth.

"Only if you want to lose," she said, picking her book back up with a grin.

His mother came into the kitchen, juggling several bottles of wine. "You're here," she said, and delight suffused her face as she gave him an air kiss on each cheek. "Sorry, I heard you calling, but I was on the phone rescheduling Janie Leopold. She has to take her mother to a doctor's appointment, and you can't do that if your head is under the hairdryer." Farrah always assumed everyone wanted the same level of gossip in their lives that her salon clients at Shear Brilliance did.

"That's okay," he said, clapping his hands. "Put me to work."

"Your father was supposed to start the grill, but he's lingering in the shower, apparently. Do you mind?"

"Nah, I don't mind. I don't really need my eyebrows, and I'm sure Kyle will patch me up if any tragedy befalls me."

"No, I won't. I've had enough work for this week."

Daniel grabbed the long matches from the drawer by the stove and went outside, only to find his oldest brother, Philip, and his sister-in-law, Claire, sitting near the fire pit on the covered patio, hands intertwined.

"Oh, I see how it is," Daniel said. "Philip's already out here, but I get put to work lighting the grill." Daniel slapped his brother on the back and gave Claire a fist bump. She was five months pregnant, and he carried enough germs around that he didn't want to risk giving her something he didn't know he had. "You guys doing okay?"

"Oh, you know," she said, rubbing her belly. "Except for the acid reflux, the constipation, and the insomnia, we're good."

"Both of you have that?" Daniel cocked his head as the grill flamed to life. "Phil, are you having sympathetic pregnancy symptoms?" He ducked as his brother threw an outdoor pillow at him, and Claire laughed. "And if you are," he continued, undeterred, "would you consider coming in to speak to my residency group about the experience?"

Philip was getting out of the chair to make Daniel shut up when he backed down. "Never mind, never mind!"

"You're all talk, baby brother." Phil smirked, sitting back down.

"Maybe not *all* talk," Daniel said thoughtfully, "but at least 75 percent." After he lit the grill, he warmed his hands over the fire for a moment. "Why are you guys sitting out here?"

"It was loud in there," Claire explained. "Also, someone else is playing with our kid."

"Ah." The sliding door opened, and his dad came outside.

"Oh good, you're here," he said, clapping him on the shoulder. "Let's go for a quick ride."

That was a no-brainer. "Sure!"

"Wait a minute," Farrah called from the kitchen. "You just went for a quick ride!"

"With Kyle, not with Daniel. Kyle doesn't know anything about bikes. Ten miles tops," Evan said, grinning, as he dragged Daniel by his collar through the kitchen toward the garage door. Daniel mouthed a quick "sorry" to his mother, who just smiled and shook her head.

"You've gotta try this," his father said, pointing to the road bike sitting in the middle of the garage.

"Which one?" Daniel asked, feigning perplexity. "How many bikes is that now? Eight?"

"I sold two of them to get this one. It's amazing. Like riding on glass."

"Sounds slippery," Daniel said, crouching down to get a better look at the gears and adjust the seat to his height.

"I got that," his dad said, grabbing an Allen wrench off the cluttered tool bench nearby. "Grab a helmet. You're gonna love it." Since his own riding gear was at his place, he blew the dust off one of his dad's loaner helmets and strapped it on. He still had his jacket on.

They headed out of town going east toward Detroit Lake, but then his dad veered onto a logging road he hadn't been down before. Daniel breathed deep and slow, letting his lungs fill completely with pine-scented air. The pavement was damp, and the forest seemed to hang on to the wet scent of rain, soak it up like a sponge. Wild rhododendrons, though not in bloom yet, broke up line after line of tall trunks. A break in the forest as they went around a curve revealed the North Santiam River. It was low this time of year, and water frothed and foamed around the large sunken rocks.

"What do you think?" his dad called over his shoulder.

"It's great," he called back, then realized his dad meant the bike. He chuckled to himself. "And the bike is great, too." He'd missed his family while he was living in Portland for med school and his first year of residency; he'd missed Timber Falls, too. As far as he was concerned, it was a great place to live at any age.

His dad was calling back stats about the bike as they went over a steel bridge with crisscrossed beams on the sides, blue-green from oxidation. There was a sign up ahead. His dad usually called those out, since he was leading, but he didn't seem to see it. Whatever, he could figure this out. *Cau-tion.* Sure, that made sense. *Caution: loo . . . loose g—* He sailed past the sign. Given a few more seconds, he would've had it. It was harder under pressure, something his second-grade teacher Mrs. Greene never figured out.

His brain filled in the missing letters with "loose girls," but he was pretty sure there were no caution signs for those. He turned to look over his shoulder, and sure enough, there was a sign on the other side with the same message. He'd get it this time: *loose gr . . . grav . . .* He didn't know if it was his attempts to look over his shoulder that undid his balance, but before he knew it, the tires had slipped out from under him, and he was skidding across the shoulder of the road on his left side. With a shout, his dad jumped off his bike and came running over.

"Are you okay? What happened?"

He was still trying to figure that out himself. Disoriented, Daniel tried to sit up, mentally measuring what hurt the most. His hip and hand were scraped, but it was his leg that felt raw and ripped like a rabid dog had gone after it.

"Just lost focus for a second," he said, wincing as his dad lifted the bike off his injured leg. *Look at that,* he thought as he looked around, *there* is *a lot of loose gravel . . . which I would've seen if I wasn't so focused on beating my dumb dyslexia.* His dad looked around, his gaze catching on the sign.

"I didn't read the sign," said Evan, his voice aggrieved. "This is my fault; I shouldn't have been so wrapped up in the bike."

"No, it's not. It's fine, it's just a scratch."

Evan placed a firm hand under his arm and helped him to his feet. "Can you make it home again on the bike?"

"Oh, yeah. Definitely." But his dad was already kneeling to examine the wound for himself, gently rolling up his torn pant leg. "Hey. Listen to the patient. I'm fine."

"Just having a quick look . . . ," Evan soothed.

"Think of it this way: this will actually be a quick ride like you promised Mom and all the other people waiting for you to grill their dinner."

"Funny bone doesn't seem to be affected," Evan muttered. "Fine, let's get you back on the bike and see how it goes."

Gingerly, Daniel mounted the bike again, the joint protesting, the pain screaming down his calf and up his thigh.

"See? I'm okay." He smiled, but his father narrowed his eyes.

"I'm not an idiot, Daniel."

"Neither am I, Dad. I don't want to sit here while you go get the car. Let's just get back to the house." The scenery didn't touch his soul in quite the same way on the way home, his pride stinging worse than the deep cuts on his knee.

CHAPTER FIVE

WINNIE WAS DREAMING about trying to set a table. The utensils kept moving while she wasn't looking, ringing against the tiles as they fell, when she suddenly realized it was her phone that was ringing. The caller ID said Jason Miller.

"Hello?"

"Hi, Winbie," said Jason. His wife, Lacey, was one of her newest patients. "I mean, Winnie. Sorry, I got distracted, I was looking at a magazine cover that used the word *newbie* in the title, and it got tangled with Winnie. I'm sorry. I do know your name, I swear . . ."

Bleary-eyed, she checked the antique clock perched on a moving box still full of comic books.

"Hi, Jason. What's happening?" It seemed like a fair question at 11:31 p.m.

"Oh right, yes. So Lacey's having some pain and cramping, and I wanted to take her to the emergency room. But she wanted me to call you first."

Smart lady. "That's good, I'm glad you did. Does she have any bleeding?" Winnie turned on the light and sat up. This wasn't going to be a phone call she could handle quickly and go back to sleep right away; there was no point in lying in the dark.

She heard him murmuring soothingly to his wife. "She says no."

"Does she have a fever?"

"No, she feels nice and cool." The octave drop in his voice told her that he'd reached out to touch her, and it made her heart feel a little loopy. Couples about to have a baby were fun to be around; despite the stress, there was a lot of tenderness in them.

"And what did she have to eat tonight?"

"She wasn't real hungry; we just had Cheerios with milk. She's been craving it a lot, with bananas. Isn't that funny? I've heard babies really like Cheerios and bananas, so it's kind of funny that the baby is already so into such things. I don't know if there's any relationship—"

"Jason," she said gently. "Can we keep the focus on Lacey for just one more minute?"

His tone was chagrined. "Yes, of course. I'm sorry. I'm just stressed."

"That's fine," Winnie said. "It's completely understandable. Is she constipated?" She put one bare foot on the distressed wooden floor to reach for her hospital bag without falling out of bed. Her notebook would remind her what Lacey had complained about last time they met. She seemed pretty easy-going; Winnie had liked her immediately.

"No, she stunk up the bathroom this morning." She heard an offended female squawk from beyond the immediate proximity of the phone, and Winnie grinned.

"What?" Jason asked. "You did."

Winnie cleared her throat, hoping to regain his attention. This one was going to be a handful as a labor coach. She'd be surprised if she could keep him in the room with Lacey; he'd probably be chasing surgery patients down the hall, wanting to chat.

"No weird smell when she pees?"

"I'm not usually there when she pees . . ."

Winnie chuckled quietly as Lacey yelled something she couldn't quite make out.

Lacey's voice came on the line, calmer now. "Hi, Winnie. Sorry about him, he's . . ." She motorboated her lips, as if baffled at how to explain her husband. "He's Jason."

"He's fine," Winnie reassured her. "Is there any chance you have a UTI?"

"No, everything seems fine, just peeing a lot."

"I realize this is a personal question, but just bear with me: Is it possible you two had sex tonight?"

"Yes, all my research said it was fine to continue having intercourse."

Winnie nodded, even though Lacey couldn't see her. "Yes, it's definitely fine, but it can sometimes prompt cramping when you . . . *finish*." She didn't consider herself a prude, but she didn't want to say "orgasm" right out loud like that. That didn't seem right. Lacey was a medical professional herself, a veterinarian; different animals, so to speak, but she had to know. Surely she could figure out what she was talking about if Winnie just leaned on the word pretty hard.

"Ah." Lacey laughed softly, and Winnie felt relief like a cool towel on the back of her neck. "I see. Well, that's good to know. Thanks for being available to answer our questions."

"Anytime. I mean that."

"Thanks, *Winbie*," Lacey teased, and she heard Jason in the background yell, "Oh, come on! It was one mistake!" They said good night and Winnie hung up. She was just getting up to use the bathroom and put away her notebook when she noticed the texts she'd missed while she was asleep.

Ethan: You up?

Ethan: I miss you, Win.

Ethan: I want to talk to you.

Ethan: Let's have lunch this week, okay? My treat.

Missed wasn't the right word; she certainly didn't miss hearing from Ethan. She hadn't blocked his number when he'd dumped her. Maybe she should have, but it didn't seem very polite to her. There could be other reasons that he'd contact her—they shared a number of mutual friends. But she would have if she'd known he was going to start texting her again. This was the third time this week, plus twice last week. Maybe if she just ignored him, he'd give it up already. It had been three months since they'd broken up; she would've expected him to be over it by now. Winnie deleted the messages and shuffled toward the bathroom.

WHEN SHE WOKE UP THE next morning, she was momentarily confused as to who was shining such a bright light on her face. *The sun.* She hadn't seen it in so long, she'd forgotten. Winnie went to the window; the sun was just cresting the top of the trees near the apartment complex, and the sky was blue and clear. Without thinking too hard, she threw on jeans and a cream cable-knit sweater. Days like this came around too infrequently to stay inside; she'd take a walk and finally explore Timber Falls' downtown . . . such as it was. Twenty minutes later, she adjusted the headband covering her ears as she descended the steps and started down the street. She could still see her breath; spring wouldn't be here for a while yet. Winnie mentally searched the yards she passed for signs of crocuses and daffodils, but it was too early. Still, it didn't hurt to be on the lookout, even in January. Really, once Christmas was over, what was the point of winter?

The trees lining the downtown were bare, their branches clacking in the stiff winter breeze. There would be tourists clogging up the sidewalks in a few months, but for now, it was all locals. She saw a few faces she recognized, but she couldn't put names to them yet. She smiled at them nonetheless. Winnie passed an antique store, an ice cream shop, a quilt store. She passed the library and waved to Starla through the window; she was the friendly librarian who'd struck up a conversation when she'd gone in to see if there was a local newspaper that might be advertising apartments for rent. Starla waved back shyly. Where Main Street crossed Hoover Avenue, there was a traffic light. It was the only one in town. When Ainsley gave her directions, she'd literally referred to it as "the light." Singular. Town Hall stood diagonal to the library, and the fire station sat between them. It was run on a volunteer basis and was very quiet this morning except for a man in yellow pants pressure-washing the moss off the driveway.

There it was: Riverside Coffee and Deli. Ainsley said they had amazing marionberry scones, and the deck overlooked the

Santiam River. It was the perfect place to enjoy a chai latte. Winnie settled into a white chair on the deck with her breakfast and her drink and was about to pull out her phone when a shadow fell over her.

"Good morning," the older woman said. "I'm Hattie. And based on the resemblance, I'd say you must be Dr. Baker's daughter."

Winnie smiled. "Yes, I am. Nice to meet you, Hattie."

"May I join you?"

She blinked. "Oh, of course. Here . . ." She pushed a chair toward her with her toe. "Please, sit down."

"Thank you," said Hattie, lowering herself slowly into the chair. She let out a happy sigh and closed her eyes, soaking in the sun. "Gotta get my vitamin D while I can, you know?"

"Yes, I certainly do, I had the same thought."

A buzzing sound drew Winnie's attention away from the woman's contented face.

"Hummingbirds," she breathed. There were ten round red feeders hung along the deck, and at least five of them were occupied, while other birds swooped and dive-bombed each other aggressively.

"Bet you didn't know they were so territorial, did you?"

"No," she said, watching with fascination as their iridescent feathers flashed in the sun.

"You're living with Ainsley Buchanan now, aren't you? How do you like it?" When Winnie's face twisted with surprise, Hattie laughed. "Hummingbirds aren't the only ones who're territorial. I like to know how things are going in my town. Just checking on you, not trying to pry. Think of me as a one-woman welcome committee."

"Well, thank you. I like it here so far."

"Glad to hear it." Hattie sipped black coffee out of a white mug that said "Timber Falls is my happy place" in black cursive. "We're glad to have another midwife around. Hope you'll stick around and take over Frances Mitton's practice." She'd gotten to work with Frances a few times, filled in for her with patients when she was attending a birth.

"I'll consider it," Winnie said, and took a big enough bite of her scone to preclude further conversation for the moment. Hattie grinned slyly as Winnie groaned. The scone *was* amazing: the tart berries paired with massive amounts of butter made it a symphony in sugar. "What is in this, magic?"

"Yup," Hattie said, settling deeper into her chair, watching the hummingbirds.

"BREATHE IN AND OUT through your nose, little sips of air," directed the thin brunette on the screen, tattoos winding around her white arms. Winnie tried to comply, but it wasn't easy when you were twisted like a pretzel, holding triangle pose. Ainsley had been trying to get Winnie to go running with her, but she kept putting her off, saying she preferred yoga. But that meant she actually had to *do* yoga instead of just talking about it. She considered just leaving the mat out conspicuously, but she didn't like untidiness.

"Three more breaths here," said the yoga instructor, and Winnie closed her eyes as her ankles wobbled, her muscles shaking. She heard a key slot into the front door just before it opened, and her eyes flew open again. Daniel stood in the doorway, mouth slightly agape, watching her with interest; after a long moment, he seemed to come to his senses.

"Hi, Winnie Baker." Daniel grinned, closing the door behind him. His hair was up, and he wore a sky-blue cashmere sweater that matched his eyes, with pressed khakis and a pair of brown vintage snakeskin loafers.

So high maintenance. Winnie tamped down her annoyance, while sending up a silent thank-you to the universe that she'd put on reasonably cute workout clothes today.

"Heard of knocking?"

"I didn't think anyone would be here, sorry."

He didn't look sorry. Not at all. In fact, he looked as happy to find her here as if he'd won the lottery—maybe not the jackpot, but one of those hundred-dollar scratch-offs at least. *Fashionable. I'm exciting for the moment, but it won't last.*

"My shift starts later today."

"Ainsley left the key under the mat so I could drop this book off for her. I guess she wants it for a lesson tomorrow or something."

"Okay, I'll get it to her." Winnie eyed the large flat brown book as he stood it up on the eat bar and she pivoted her triangle to the other leg. On the cover was a sepia illustration of a man in a suit with a suitcase, staring down at a white cat-like creature. "Aren't you a grown man? What are you doing with a picture book, anyway?"

He crossed his arms over his chest and scowled at her playfully, lowering his voice a full octave. "Don't make me angry; you wouldn't like me when I'm angry."

Winnie peered at him over her bent right knee, forgetting all about looking at the eye of her elbow like she was supposed to. "Are you quoting the Hulk right now?"

His eyes widened. "Yes! Winnie Baker, you know the Hulk's catchphrase?"

She unbent herself and the blood rushed away from her head. "Doesn't everyone?"

"No! Not by a long shot. You wouldn't believe how many blank stares I get. But don't worry, I don't actually have much of a temper. I leave the smashing and trashing to others. Unless you're trashing graphic novels, and then you should be prepared for a stern, nonviolent talking-to."

"I wasn't trashing them. I was just curious." She chose not to mention the hundreds of comic books that sat in her bedroom, encased in plastic, boxed to keep them away from the light. "I assume your skin doesn't turn green."

"Unfortunately, no, but can you imagine how popular I'd be if it did? It'd be epic."

"Come to Santiam Hospital, get treated by a gentle green doctor. Is that it?"

His gaze softened. "That's it. Hey, any chance you're free for dinner tonight?"

"I'm afraid not. Perhaps another time." She *had* promised Ainsley and Martina they would watch a movie tonight, but really, she was just being polite suggesting he still had a chance; surely he'd understand that.

He smiled. "Okay." Daniel cleared his throat, gesturing over his shoulder with one thumb. "I'll leave you to finish your workout in peace. Nice to see you again."

Winnie turned her attention back to her practice, but her concentration was off. She was remembering...

"Whatcha reading, sweet pea?" She turned to see her dad wander into the living room with several books in his arms. He angled his head to see better. "Captain Underpants?" She grinned as he made a face. "Oh, we can do better than that. Come with me."

His office? She wasn't allowed in here. With fascination, she followed him into the darkened room to a shelf filled with thin books.

"Let's see, what's kid-appropriate . . . ," he mumbled to himself. "Ah. Here. The Hulk, that should be okay. Read this and let me know what you think. There's a lot more where that comes from."

"What does he do?" she asked, flipping through it, touching the bright colors on the pages.

"Wait until they make Hulk mad. You find out. Hulk have bad temper." He flexed his biceps and stuck out his jaw, and Winnie laughed.

When she finished the video, she padded back to her room on bare feet on the thin carpet. Kneeling, she took the lid off the box of comics . . . It should be here somewhere. With a triumphant flourish, she pulled out *Incredible Hulk* #24. She would lose herself in the book for a while in order to not think about the handsome doctor who'd dropped by so unexpectedly, who apparently shared her affinity for her favorite art form; Bruce needed to avenge his murdered wife, after all. The Abomination must be defeated. The corners of the pages were discolored and bent; she'd read this one so many times after her dad died. It was a way to remember him, to remember the good times they'd had. His love of books, his silly faces, the way he could captivate a room with a story, how he was mild mannered to a fault. Reading these pages over and over, she'd wished there were some way to find closure. Wished there were someone she could battle in retaliation for losing him too soon.

CHAPTER SIX

"THERE SHE IS," HER grandfather bellowed when he opened the front door. "There she is, oh, come here, you." He wrapped her in a hug that squeezed the air out of her lungs and that didn't stop until she tipped her head to kiss his rough cheek. Howard smelled like coffee and cigars tonight. He was wearing the kind of pinstriped dress shirt he wore to teach his economics classes at Oregon State, not his usual Sunday casual.

"What are we watching?"

"Seahawks at Broncos."

"Ooh, you must feel torn."

"I do, child," he said, nodding somberly, pressing a hand over his heart. "I do. Thank you for understanding. Rooting for the team of one's childhood home is sacred." His greeting for her mother was nearly as enthusiastic, though he released her much earlier. He called her "child" as well, kissing her cheek. Her dad's family had always been a bit demonstrative, her mother had explained to her as a child. *Just go with it,* she'd whispered. *You can always fix your hair later.*

Winnie was slipping off her shoes and hanging up her coat when she heard her grandmother singing. She'd always admired her voice, and she'd had ample opportunity to hear it: when Heloise Baker wanted music, she largely made it herself.

For tonight's selection, however, she was allowing her speakers to accompany her, even though it was an old favorite: "Una Notte a Napoli" by Pink Martini. The sweeping, romantic music always made Winnie wish she knew how to ballroom dance. Its sustained minor key was wistful.

"Darling! You're here!" Heloise said, letting the music go on without her. "How are you? Isn't this a wonderful piece? I'm making osso bucco, I felt it was only right."

"It's perfect," Winnie assured her, winding an arm behind Heloise for a tight shoulder squeeze. "And it smells delicious."

"I made ciabatta bread, too; I know how you love that, Sandy." No one else dared to call Sandra Baker such a warm nickname, but her father had used it, and her grandparents seemed to have picked it up in his absence. Her mother simply nodded. Apparently, she didn't feel like informing them that she'd basically stopped eating carbs years ago.

"Can I make a salad or anything?" Winnie asked, washing her hands in the kitchen sink.

"Of course," Heloise answered. Winnie was pulling out radicchio and English cucumbers and all sorts in no time. Her grandmother always had such fun veggies; what the heck was this weird root vegetable?

"Are these carrots?"

She nodded. "Purple carrots, yes. They were in our CSA box." Sandra and Howard shared an eye roll which Heloise caught as she spooned sauce over the veal.

"Don't start, you two," Heloise chided. "I love my CSA box. I don't mind eating a lot of brussels sprouts."

"Brussels sprouts for days," Howard quipped, pouring himself a glass of red wine. "Winnie, you want some wine? Sandra?"

"No, thank you, we're fine."

Winnie turned her back to her mother in order to find a cutting board, trying to ignore the pinch of irritation at not being allowed to answer for herself. She did have a lot of patients who were close to their due dates, she reasoned. That was probably the reason her mother had answered preemptively. She listened with half an ear as her mother filled her in-laws in on the happenings at the hospital. The mention of Daniel's name, however, had both ears listening.

"His father and his brother have both proven to be very capable physicians, I have no doubt he will as well. Just needs to grow up a bit, I suppose. He touches the patients often."

"What's wrong with that?" Howard asked, pulling down pewter plates.

"Nothing, I suppose. Just a different style to mine. Not very professional, though."

"He's not inappropriate, though, is he?" Winnie asked. She couldn't help but think back to their initial encounter . . . He'd come on strong. Very strong.

"No, not inappropriate. But doctors have to maintain some emotional distance. He seems to get very wrapped up in his patients' situations. I caught him picking the dead flowers out of Mrs. Redding's bouquet while she was asleep after she'd complained about them."

"Sounds very considerate to me," Heloise commented, carrying the red Dutch oven to the table, the contents still bubbling.

"But there are better uses of his valuable time," Sandra replied. "At any rate, I'm sure he'll soon learn."

Winnie had little doubt of that. She'd seen her mother's mentoring ruin the compassion of several young doctors over the years. And now that she had a residency program, she was getting them even younger. Daniel, she thought, stood a decent chance at staying tenderhearted; if his pursuit of her was any indication, he had an unnatural willingness to persevere despite the odds against him. Little thoughts, the kind she often felt forced by her upbringing to ignore, began to filter in like dandelion seeds carried on a stiff breeze. Little thoughts that suggested being an ally to him might even the odds a bit, that she might whisper hope to a young doctor.

"Winifred, I forgot to tell you—you had some mail come to the house. One piece looked particularly important: a wedding invitation."

"From whom?"

Her mother sipped her water. "The return address said Weaver."

"Kari Weaver? My professor at OHSU?"

"I would presume so. You were quite close, weren't you?" She knew they had been. Winnie had been her teaching assistant the summer after she graduated. Kari had been more than a professor; she'd been a mentor in every sense of the word. She'd impressed Winnie from their first meeting. Dr. Weaver shared her passion for effective treatment that stretched beyond traditional Western medicine. And she'd introduced her to strawberry honey balsamic ice cream with black pepper at Salt and Straw . . . She'd changed her life in so many ways. If Dr. Weaver was getting married, she would definitely go.

But so would Ethan, her ex; Dr. Weaver and Ethan were related, albeit distantly. A second cousin, if memory served. The thought of seeing him again was unwelcome, especially somewhere as romantic as a wedding. They'd talked about getting married, a little. Enough that she'd started pinning color schemes on Pinterest . . . dusty blue and gold. She would definitely need a buffer, someone to fend off his attention; she was not going down that path with him again. Not after what he'd said.

"Winnie?" her mother said softly. "Isn't that the professor you admired so much, the one with all the *interesting* ideas about natural childbirth?" Her mother and grandparents were all watching her quizzically, like her cat when he used to watch *Planet Earth*.

"I'd say 'progressive,' not 'interesting,' but yes, Dr. Weaver and I were quite close, and we've kept in touch despite the Ethan . . ." She searched for the right word. ". . . debacle."

Sandra stabbed at a cucumber. "I still can't imagine what you did to drive him away like that."

Winnie bristled. "I didn't do anything. We were on different paths, that's all."

"Did you tell him you're taking the MCATs again?"

She caught the way her grandmother's head lifted sharply out of the corner of her eye, and she made herself raise her gaze to meet Heloise's directly. "No, I didn't."

"Perhaps if he knew you haven't given up yet, it would—"

"Mom. I'd rather not talk about this right now."

"Fine."

"Who wants coffee?" Heloise asked, rising from the table. "Winnie, will you help me with the cheesecake, please?"

"Of course." She patted her mouth with her white cotton napkin, stalling, as her grandmother disappeared into the kitchen. The hallway wasn't long enough for her to figure out what to say either. Heloise dropped the pretense of dessert entirely now that they were out of earshot. Arms braced behind her on the counters, her steely blue gaze bore into her.

"Winnie, why does your mother think you're taking the MCATs again?"

She looked up at the ceiling. "Because I told her I would."

"Why?" she hissed. "Please, please don't do this to yourself, darling. You're such a smart girl. I don't see why you're putting yourself through this again. You love what you do, don't you?"

"Yes," Winnie murmured, wanting to massage the pain from her own temples.

"So I say again: Why are you taking the MCATs?"

"It'll make her happy, Grandma."

"No, it won't. I love your mother, Winnie, you know I do, but you going to medical school is just exchanging your future happiness for someone else's extremely temporary satisfaction. It will not change the fact that your father is gone." She handed her a stack of red china plates and forks. "Tell her the truth, darling."

Winnie nodded noncommittally, trying to give her grandmother a reassuring smile, but Heloise's face stayed sad and concerned as she turned to get the cake from the fridge. A sick feeling slithered around in her stomach. Maybe she'd skip dessert after all.

CHAPTER SEVEN

ON WEDNESDAY, DANIEL was finishing his yogurt and icing his elevated leg when Kyle came into the on-call room and slumped onto the couch next to him.

"Rough day?"

Kyle ran a hand through his dark hair. "Referral to oncology."

He swallowed down his bite and the sadness that welled up. "Yikes. Anyone I know?"

"Mavis Johnson."

"Oh, that's sad." She'd worked at the library for years. He loved the library; he'd gotten kicked out for being rowdy and noisy more times than he could count, but she'd always been nice about it. The clock caught his eye. "I'll have to go by and check on her later. Is she still here?"

"Nope, she wanted to get back to the library by three for when school gets out."

"What time is it? Ooh, it's almost two. You know what that means," Daniel said.

"No."

Daniel made his eyebrows dance. "It's flirting time." Daniel limped over to the nurse's station and Kyle followed reluctantly.

"Hey there, Miss Baker."

She didn't look up. "Hello, Thor. Loki."

He wanted to see her eyes. What could he say to get her to look up?

"Am I Thor because of my resemblance to Chris Hemsworth, because I'm a god, or because you suspect I have a secret identity?"

"None of the above; it's because you're a limping doctor with a wicked brother."

"She didn't deny that I'm handsome," he whispered too loudly to Kyle, who gave him an incredulous look. Those looks didn't bother him anymore. "Kyle's not wicked, though, Winnie. He's just broody."

Kyle crossed his arms over his chest. "I'm going to assume this is some kind of superhero reference."

"Loki is Thor's morally ambiguous brother, always trying to get the upper hand."

"Well, that's faulty, then. I've already got the upper hand."

Kyle moved away from the station, and Daniel called after him. "That's such a Loki thing to say!"

He waved at him without turning around. Daniel turned back to Winnie. "If I'm Thor, where's my hammer?"

"I just assumed you kept it in your locker during work hours." Winnie popped the chart she was holding into the file and closed the file cabinet quietly, then turned down the floor. "No one can steal it anyway."

Best as he could, Daniel chased Winnie. "Am I the Marvel universe Thor or DC Comics?"

Winnie tapped a pen to her lips. "Marvel, I'd say. Definitely not Neil Gaiman's. You're not drunk enough."

"Does that make you Jane Foster?"

He watched Winnie's face fall. "I don't think so." *Is that a bad thing? Why did that make her sad?*

"The parallels are clearly there: you're a nurse who wants to be a doctor, worthy to wield Mjölnir."

She reached room 213, then stopped to face him. "What makes you think I'd be worthy?"

His head was full of things he couldn't say yet: *Because I dream about how pretty you are. Because I've seen you with your patients, and your patience and integrity is amazing. Because you seem to carry the weight of the world with ease.* He opted for a safer route than baring his soul.

"What makes you think you wouldn't be?"

She pursed her lips. Was she hiding a smile? Oh, definitely.

"I don't know why I talk to you. You just ask ridiculous questions."

Daniel grinned at her. "Because I'm funny. Because you like it."

Winnie looked him up and down, and her gaze seemed to catch on his leg. "You're limping. Why?"

He scratched his chin thoughtfully. "I thought it would give me character. I'm trying out different distinguishing characteristics. Next, I'm going to grow a mustache, and then I'll try a hat. I was thinking of a beret."

Winnie regarded him skeptically. "First of all, you'd look terrible in a beret, so I certainly hope you're joking." She gestured insistently toward his leg. "What did you do to yourself? Or was this at the hands of another? A wicked brother, maybe?"

"Oh, no, nothing like that." He ran a hand over his bound hair. "Cycling accident." Her eyes widened adorably, and he could tell she was imagining all sorts of terrible circumstances that this might entail. "I'm just a little scraped up, really. I'm fine. I was just icing it. The gravel was loose and I went down hard, but . . ."

"Let me see."

He sighed. This was the thing about being in relationships with medical professionals: they *all* wanted to see. It was like they didn't trust him to diagnose himself correctly, or maybe they just needed to assuage their curiosity. Whatever the case, he'd already endured his father's examination and later, his brother's . . . Yet somehow, he didn't mind Winnie's scrutiny as much as theirs. Still, it could be fun to pretend he did.

"All right," he said, holding up his hands, "but you'll make it quick, won't you?" He led her farther down the hall. "I'm a very busy, important doctor. Mr. Helsing is counting on me to bring him candy, and Mrs. Mapleton said she wanted me to take out her stitches, because I have a lighter touch. Personally, I think it might have more to do with my studly physique, but I could be misreading the situation."

As he talked, she pulled him into an empty exam room by his sleeve and shut the door, then washed her hands at the sink. When he sat down in one of the chairs, she tilted her head toward the exam table as she dried her hands.

"Really, Nurse Baker?" He didn't particularly want to get up on the table . . . yet he wanted to spend time alone with her and see where he could take it.

"Really, Dr. Durand. The light is better. It's more sanitary. And more than that, it's closer to my face. I don't get down on the floor unless absolutely necessary."

"I've seen you on the floor for less-than-necessary reasons," he said, and her gaze narrowed. Maybe she could tell that he'd thought about opening the apartment door to find her standing like a warrior, her muscles taut and strong, about a hundred times since then, often while he was in the shower. He just skipped the painful part when she shot him down.

"Fine, fine," he laughed. "I surrender."

He pulled the pant leg of his gray slacks up to his knee. Her fingers skirted over the long contusion down the side of his leg; they were cold, and he had to make himself stay still. She was wholly focused on examining him, which gave him a moment to imagine her long hair let down, wavy. It was so thick and his fingers itched to weave themselves into it just to see how it felt.

"You didn't get all the gravel out of this," she said, frowning.

"What?" He'd kind of forgotten what they were supposed to be doing. "Really?" That was unlikely, given that two people had looked at it already.

"Really." The unmistakable snap of her putting on a glove startled him.

"Oh, you don't have to take it out, I can do it."

"It'll be easier if I do it," she said, grabbing a pair of tweezers from her bag that he hoped were clean. They probably were. He didn't know why it was making him so nervous to have her working on him; she was a total professional. It wasn't her skills. It was just . . . her. So quiet, so focused. So . . . persuasive. She rested her left hand, ungloved, on his leg as she went to work with her tool of choice; her touch was calming and exciting at the same time.

Plink. Speaking of distraction, more tiny gravel fragments bounced against the metal as she dropped them in the pan. He opened his mouth to protest again, but she was already asking him a question he hadn't been listening to.

"Do you know where I got these tweezers?"

"Um. No?"

"These are not just normal tweezers. They're insanely pointed on the ends and perfect for getting small fragments out from under the skin." *Plink.* "I got them at a quilt store in Sisters. Not that I have much call for removing small fragments in the course of my normal work with mothers. But it's nice to have the option when the situation calls for it." She straightened, apparently satisfied with her work on his leg, and she sprayed it with a bottle of antiseptic spray she apparently also had in her bag. Winnie patted his leg. "All done."

"Thank you," he said meekly.

"You're welcome," she said, very businesslike. He expected her to open the door, but she didn't. Eyes on her bag, she continued talking.

"Earlier, you mentioned that I wanted to be a doctor. How did you know that?"

"Your mother mentioned it during one of her lectures."

Winnie nodded slowly, still reorganizing her bag. He rolled his pant leg down as he watched her carefully. She wasn't looking at him, so it was hard to read her expression exactly ... but it felt like dismay. Something wasn't right, and that cryptic expression was making him curious ...

"Don't you?" he asked softly.

"Don't I what?"

"Want to be a doctor?"

She slung her bag over her shoulder, her expression sour. *Oops, that wasn't the right thing to say.*

"I can't see how that's any of your business." She moved for the door, but he caught her arm gently.

"Hey. Winnie. I didn't mean to pry. I thought it was public knowledge."

"It's public knowledge that I've failed the MCATs five times consecutively. I just didn't realize my mother was spreading the idea that I'm still trying."

Daniel knew from his friendship with Ainsley and his closeness with his sister Maggie that he needed to tread carefully on such a delicate subject. "Aren't you happy being a midwife?"

She pivoted to face him. "Yes, I am."

It would be a mistake to mention her age here . . . but he couldn't think of anything else to say.

Winnie smiled. "Yes, I would be an old medical school student. You can say it, whippersnapper."

He threw his hands up in mock disgust. "I'm not that much older than you!"

"Oh, really? How many kids were in *The Brady Bunch*?"

"Six. Three boys, three girls."

"That was a warm-up question. On *Perfect Strangers*, where was Balki from?"

"Who?"

"Who played Mork in the classic TV show *Mork & Mindy*?"

"Tom Hanks?"

Winnie nodded, as if congratulating herself. "That's what I thought."

"Wait, you didn't watch that stuff when it came out."

She had the grace to blush a little. "No, I saw it in reruns. But so what?"

"Winnie, this is what IMDb is for. And I can watch all that stuff on some streaming service."

She poked a finger gently into his chest, and her eyes flared at the contact with his firm muscles there. In a flash, it was gone, but it filled him with gratification nonetheless. "My point isn't that you couldn't watch it now, my point is that you didn't watch it *then*. My point is that I'm significantly older than you."

"You watched it in reruns; you may be older than me, but it's not significant. At least not to me."

Winnie gave him a flat smile. "Then you're the only one."

CHAPTER EIGHT

NACHOS. WHEN SHE WAS done with this delivery, Winnie was totally going to make nachos, loaded with black olives, avocado, sour cream, pico de gallo salsa. No cilantro, though. She could barely stand it when Ainsley used it in the apartment.

Her patient, Darby, groaned as her next contraction hit. She was bouncing gently on the large orange exercise ball, her long brown hair swaying, sweaty near her temples. Darby was close to transition now. She'd been walking the hallways of the hospital for the last few hours, alongside her child's father. It was hard to tell exactly what their relationship was . . . Shane hadn't been to any of her prenatal checkups, but he was here now, so he obviously cared.

"You're doing great, D," he murmured, rubbing her shoulders, but she shook him off. Even under his scruffy beard, the kind that looked unintentional, Winnie could see how disappointed he was to have his comfort rejected. Maybe he'd noticed what Winnie had also seen: the mother was tensing her whole body with every spasm, rather than letting the pain wash over her. She was fighting the change, fighting the pain, treating it like humans were taught to treat pain: a sign that something was wrong. That wasn't a helpful mindset during labor. Winnie lived for times like this, when she could really be present with a patient, instead of needing to bounce between rooms. She'd also done some training as a doula, and she liked being able to guide women, help them find their own way through a birth experience.

"Darby," she said, "you are totally doing great. What would help you relax between contractions?" Without asking, she picked up the young woman's hand and began to massage it. Shane was watching carefully, and she gave him a wide-eyed, meaningful look, hoping to communicate that this would be a better place for him to try to massage her if she was feeling averse to touch at the moment.

"I don't know," Darby said, her voice small. She wiped the sweat from her forehead with her shoulder. "I'm just so tired."

"I know," Winnie assured her. "You're working hard, but don't work harder than you have to. Try to rest between contractions. Would you like to lie down?"

"No, it'll go faster if I'm upright. If I lie down, I won't be able to get back up."

Winnie doubted that, but she didn't want to argue with her. "Okay, you can stay here for now. But I notice that the contractions are coming closer together, which hopefully means you're headed toward transition, and we're going to want you closer to the bed when you start to deliver, okay?" She patted her hand. "I'm going to go check on another patient. I'll be right back. Would you like Shane to hold your hand?"

She nodded, and Shane slipped into the rocking chair she vacated, taking Darby's hand in both of his. Winnie left quietly as the two looked at each other with fear and anticipation, like they knew life was changing forever right now, and she smiled to herself. In truth, she just needed to use the bathroom and grab a snack, and she didn't want to use the one in their room. It was good to give couples, even couples as loosely affiliated as this one, time together before everything really got started. Down the hall, she spotted Dr. Durand—the other one; she never seemed to see Kyle around for some reason, and their dad had his own clinic in Timber Falls. He was talking with Martina, so she turned the other way to hide her face and ducked into a storage room. She didn't want him asking any more questions about her future plans. If she could just hold on a little longer, her mother would certainly give up soon. She didn't need him announcing to Dr. Baker that she was a fake and a fraud. And yet, she thought, as she stacked the toilet paper on the shelf in front of her more neatly, she'd enjoyed talking to him until the conversation had taken a turn toward her becoming a doctor. They could be friends, surely, if only because of Ainsley.

Winnie cracked open the solid door of the storage closet, cursing herself for picking a room without a window on the door. The coast appeared to be clear. She turned to shut the door quietly, then ran directly into a white-coated chest.

"I thought I saw you go in there. Didn't want to scare you by coming in after you."

"Oh, I'm sorry, I—"

"It's okay, Nurse Baker. Bumping into people is just something that happens later at night." Daniel smiled down at her. "Don't you think?"

"I suppose so," she said, unable to keep a hand from running over the ponytail she'd put up hours ago that was probably falling out. *Why do I care what I look like? I'm almost a decade older than this man.* She groped for something meaningful to say. "Working swing tonight?" *Genius, Winifred.*

"Nah. I just like to hang out here hoping cute midwives will bump into me," he said, his grin widening even more.

Winnie rubbed her nose. "I'm not cute."

"No?" His eyes flashed at the challenge.

"No. And I'm about to be even less cute when I've got fluid all over my shoes."

"Hmm, you make a good point. But stop by and find me before you leave, and I'll give you an unbiased assessment."

Ethan's face, twisted in disgust, flashed into her mind. He'd stopped by her mother's home to drop off an article he thought she'd enjoy and caught her before she'd cleaned up all the way after a home birth. She'd hated that feeling, the way it diminished something that lit up her life. The way it cast a shadow on a beautiful morning. She always showered at the hospital now, when she was done.

"I don't think you'll care for it, but if I remember, I will stop by and let you see for yourself." Winnie gave him half a smile, then turned back to Darby's room, unwrapping the protein bar she'd had in her pocket as she retraced her path down the hall. What she saw through the window of the door made her stomach clench. Winnie opened the door quietly, stealthily, and caught just the end of the conversation.

"It's not too late yet for an anesthesiologist," her mother was saying. "Dr. Waters is on call tonight, and he's one of our best. I just saw him down the hall, but I could—"

"Dr. Baker." She kept her voice unconcerned, light. Her mother pivoted to her, but didn't move toward the door. Darby's expression was dark, and Winnie could tell she was upset. She crossed to her patient and knelt next to her.

"I'm sorry about this, Darby. I'll get this straightened out and be right back. It won't happen again." Her patient nodded, clearly relieved. She stood and shifted her attention to her mother. "I need to speak with you outside, please."

As soon as the door closed, Winnie wanted to round on her. Wanted to wipe that "this should be good" expression off her pastel face. She forced herself to take a deep breath and hold it to the count of ten before she slowly released it through her nose, leaning into the feeling of fresh oxygen in her tired brain.

"What are you doing down here?"

"Babies are part of family medicine. Things are slow upstairs at this time of night."

Winnie flexed her jaw. "Dr. Baker, this patient's birth plan made it clear that she wished to deliver naturally. Did you consult her birth plan?"

"What did she do, download a form from Baby Center?" Sandra shook her head lightly, a quiet condemnation, but a condemnation nonetheless.

"It was WhatToExpect.com, I believe. Either way, you have no right or authority to go against her wishes. You would never disregard a DNR. I don't see how this is any different."

Her mother calmly stuck her hands in the pockets of her white coat. "A DNR is life and death, so I do believe it's somewhat different. I was just informing her of her options. That's all."

Winnie, being fully aware of her mother's prejudices against natural childbirth, crossed her arms over her chest. "I will be responsible for making her aware of her options. Please stay out of my patient's room, especially when I'm not there."

"Just didn't want to hear her shrieking in pain when there was a solution available to her . . ."

"She's not—" Darby's high cry cut her off, and Winnie winced. She must be in transition; she was never going to make any real progress with those high, unproductive yells. Winnie yanked open the door, but turned to look over her shoulder and give her mother another warning look. Sandra put her hands up in a show of innocence, then turned and left without another word.

CHAPTER NINE

IT WAS ALMOST SUNRISE, and Daniel was finishing handing off his patients to the next shift. Dr. Baker had been in a bad mood most of the evening, so he figured she wouldn't mind if he just passed them off himself. Neither she nor Winnie was anywhere to be found. He figured she'd probably already finished her birth and left. He was trying not to feel too disappointed about it, like a kid who knew two scoops of ice cream was too much for that tiny sugar cone and consoles himself with the idea that he knew the chocolate one was going to fall.

"And here we have Mrs. Renfro, who sewed through her finger."

Greg Trout looked disturbed. "How did that happen?"

Daniel didn't get a chance to answer.

"Well, my niece, she's having a baby, you see, just upstairs, and I was trying like mad to get the baby quilt I'm making her done before her little one arrives. And I got distracted for just a moment when the bratty sister on that royalty show—the British one, you know—she was just about to take off her clothes for that photographer—you know, the scandalous one—" His phone buzzed.

Kyle: You done?

He and his brother had driven to work together, and he would now be waiting for him. Kyle hated waiting. Mrs. Renfro was still talking.

"And I thought about waking up Foster, but he'd just gotten back from a long-haul run to Las Vegas—you know, Sin City—and he was so tired, so I just got in my car, and—"

"And gave me the opportunity to take my first 90/14 quilting machine needle out of an index finger," Daniel said quickly, trying to wrestle the conversation back as gently as he could.

"I was afraid to pull it out myself," Mrs. Renfro explained, holding out her injured hand so they could see the damage.

Kyle: Hello?

Daniel: Be right there.

"She hadn't had a tetanus shot in a while, so we got that done..."

"Didn't even get any blood on the fabric," she boasted. "It's going to be beautiful."

Kyle: Where are you?

"But she should be ready to be discharged as soon as her husband gets here." He turned so that he was facing away from Mrs. Renfro and lowered his voice. "She was a little hysterical when she got here, so we had to give her a mild sedative. Don't let her drive home alone."

"Gotcha." Greg smiled, turning back to Mrs. Renfro. "All right, Pamela, I'll check on those discharge papers for you. Dr. Durand's got to run on home now."

Kyle: Earth to Danny...

Daniel: I'm coming, I'm coming.

He was grimacing at the nickname he'd outgrown in third grade when he stepped out into the hallway and saw a very tired Winifred coming his way, eyes shining, hair wet, flip-flops on, giant bag slung across her chest, bouncing against her back. How she still managed to look so great, he'd never know. Yes, there were bags under her eyes and a definite slower pace to her walk, but she was smiling to herself, and the quiet joy of her took his breath away.

"Nope," he called, and she looked up sharply. "Still cute. Sorry."

She gave him a real smile as she slowed to a stop in front of him. "This doesn't count. I already showered, and my other shoes are in my bag, carefully wrapped in plastic to contain the grossness."

Winnie was gazing up at him, biting her lip, still smiling like someone had turned on a light inside her. Her teeth against that petal-pink skin . . . It made him forget what he wanted to say. It made him want to kiss her gently, touch the soft skin of her cheeks, stroke the gold of her hair. It made him a little light-headed.

His phone rang, and he answered it without breaking their staring contest. "Yeah?"

"Are you coming or what?" Kyle asked. "I'm beat. I want to go home."

A thought formed in Daniel's mind, and he was self-aware enough to realize that his lack of sleep might be creating crack-pot ideas in his brain . . . but maybe it was worth a try.

"I think Winnie's going to give me a ride."

"Fine. See you later." Kyle hung up.

"You might've asked me first," she said, raising one blonde eyebrow.

"Do you mind? I'm going to your apartment; Ainsley needs help building a theatre for puppets or something."

"Oh," Winnie said, turning toward the locker room, "is that what all that lumber was for? I wondered."

"Did she at least get a kit?"

"Didn't look like it. And you'll have to be outside. I need sleep."

"She probably hasn't thought that through . . ." Daniel sighed. "You wanna drive through Rico's?"

Winnie stopped suddenly. "How did you know I was craving nachos?"

"I didn't. Lucky guess. Kyle and I like to swing by there after work. Good breakfast burritos."

She held up a hand. "Say no more. Get your stuff. I'll be in the car." Daniel ducked into the changing room only to grab his backpack, but when he got to the parking lot, he found himself slowing to a stop. He had no idea what her car looked like. A dark-blue Corolla flashed its lights, and he grinned. There were some fir twigs strewn across the gravel parking lot as he crossed it, and it made him realize how out of it he was; he hadn't even heard the wind in the night. Maybe he shouldn't be operating power tools this morning, but he'd already promised.

The line at Rico's wasn't long, but the silence in the car between them once they'd ordered was. He had her alone—finally. He wanted to talk to her, to impress her. But his tired brain just wasn't cooperating. He'd have to settle for small talk.

"Where are you from?"

"Northern California, originally," Winnie said, running a hand through her wet hair.

Daniel winced. "Oh dear."

"I know. It made me an instant object of scorn and ridicule in school."

"I can imagine."

"Oregonians really hate Californians, don't they?"

"I'm afraid so. It runs deep. It may actually be deeper than hate . . . Is *loathing* a word?"

"I believe it is, but I'm so tired, I can't be sure." Winnie smiled.

"Same. At least you're from Northern California. That's a little more forgivable. They're more crunchy, like us. At least you're not from LA."

"Mom wouldn't be caught dead in LA. We have standards."

They pulled forward and, salivating, received their long-awaited food. The smell of eggs, salsa, and cheddar filled the car.

"Oh, that smells amazing," Winnie moaned. "I want it now. But I can't drive and eat."

Daniel paused in unwrapping his burrito as she pulled out of the parking lot. "Pull over, we'll switch. I don't care. Mine'll keep, yours is going to get soggy."

Winnie gave him the side-eye. "I can't let you drive my car. We barely know each other."

I'd really, really like to know you, though, he thought as he took a huge bite. Still, driving her car would probably be seen as possessive and relationship-y by anyone who saw them. And he knew someone from the town would see, and then they'd mention it casually (read: pointedly) under the hair dryer at Shear Brilliance, and then his mother would know. And then he'd get grilled.

"Why'd you guys move to Oregon, then? Your dad get a job here or something?"

She focused on the road. "My mom, actually. And my grandparents, my dad's parents, are here."

He frowned. "Do I know them?"

"Heloise and Howard Baker?"

"Not ringing a bell," he said between bites. *Sweet potatoes. Sweet potatoes are amazing. This burrito is amazing.*

"They live in Lyons," she said, turning onto the highway going east. "Mom wanted to be closer to Salem for the schools."

"Hey, what's wrong with our schools? Coop knows all twenty-three letters of the alphabet already!"

She laughed softly. "Who's Coop?"

"My brother Philip's kid. You know Claire at the hospital? She's an admin?"

Winnie nodded.

"That's his wife. They've been married a couple of years. She's pretty cool."

"And how old is Cooper? I assume it's Cooper and not some strange, hippy amalgamation of a name."

"Yes, it's Cooper, and he's five. Just started kindergarten, and I thought my brother was going to have a fit in the days leading up. Parents are weird."

"His son was nervous?"

"No, *Philip* was nervous. Cooper was fine. Cooper's always fine; that kid can roll with it like a pro wrestler. He'll make a great doctor someday."

Winnie kept looking over at his side of the car, but she wasn't looking at his face. She was looking at the brown paper bag on his lap, damp with condensation from the hot food trapped inside.

"How do you know he'll be a doctor?"

"All Durands are doctors," he said, unwrapping the paper on his breakfast a bit more. "It's in our blood."

"Your brother's not," she pointed out.

He tipped his head, conceding the point. "No, Philip's kind of the black sheep, but he's still in medicine; he's a physical therapist." He started to take another bite, then stopped. "Wait, no. *Maggie's* the black sheep," he said, chuckling.

"Why, what does Maggie do?"

"Nothing she doesn't want to. She's still in high school. She's just contrary as the day is long. Wants nothing to do with medicine whatsoever." He took his bite and talked through it. "Sorry, I'm just dying of starvation. What about you? Is your dad a doctor? Your siblings?"

"I don't have any siblings, and my dad was an English professor."

He nodded slowly. "Was?"

"Yes. He died when I was ten. Heart attack."

He felt like he'd swallowed a lead ball. "That sucks."

She shrugged. "It did. He ran marathons, he always ate right. It was a total shock, but what can you do?"

"Nothing," he said, shaking his head, and he let his hands fall to his lap, his stomach feeling sour. "That sucks, Winnie. I'm sorry."

Her gaze dropped to the bag again.

"I see you pining for your nachos," he teased, grateful for an opportunity to change the subject. He didn't like to see her sad.

"Just let me open them for you, and you can pick at them while you drive."

Winnie licked her lips, and he grinned. "No, no," she said, almost as if she was arguing with herself. "I can't. I don't eat while I drive. It'll spill and make a mess."

Daniel pulled out the plastic container that held the nachos and removed the clear lid, inhaling deeply just over the surface of the cheese. "Sure smells good."

"Stop that." She was weakening. He could hear it in her voice, and he filed that timbre away for later, when she might be weakening similarly in her resolve regarding . . . other things.

"It's gonna get soggy," he said, wafting the scent toward her with the lid. "Just one chip."

"No." She scowled. "We're almost there."

"Your self-control is admirable," he said, plucking a chip from the container and popping it into his mouth.

Winnie's guttural outrage startled him. "Did you just eat my chip? Daniel Durand, that is MY food! Do not put your dirty hands on my food!"

"Dirty?" he asked, still chewing. "I'm a doctor. I'm always clean."

"Disgusting. Seriously."

"I only touched the one I took, I promise."

"I want to take your word for it, but . . ."

"You can totally take my word for it. I promise. Your food is un-germified," he said as they pulled into Winnie's designated spot under the carport. "Here," he said, covering the food as he passed it to her. "It's all yours."

"It better be," she mumbled as she shoved three chips into her mouth. "So good," she groaned.

He opened the car door and stuck one leg out. "You coming inside?"

"In a minute," she sighed. "So tired."

"I'll get your bag for you," he said, heaving his body out of the economy car and dragging himself to the back. She must have been fine with that, because she popped the trunk. He tried to lift the bag to his shoulder, but he stumbled at the additional weight all on one side. "Good Lord, woman. What is in this bag?"

"Everything," she yawned. "Everything you need to bring a new person into the world, it's in that bag." They both staggered up the two flights of outdoor stairs and Winnie led the way into the apartment.

"Hello?" she called. "Ainsley?" Hearing no response, Winnie shuffled down the hall toward the bedrooms, still softly calling her roommate's name. When she reappeared, her face was pinched with worry. "I don't think she's here. I'm sorry."

Daniel shook his head, grinning. Of course she forgot. And of course Winnie would apologize for someone else's mistake. "Don't worry about it. She's been standing me up for years now. She'll remember at eight tomorrow night, most likely, when she slows down enough to look at her calendar." He sat down hard on their slate-gray couch. "I'll call Kyle. He'll bitch about it, but he'll come get me."

"Oh, I can run you home."

"You sure? Because it's possible Kyle is already asleep. God knows I would be if I were home right now."

Winnie nodded. "Just let me eat first. I'll just be a few minutes."

He should go sit next to her on a hard stool and make polite conversation while she finished her breakfast, but he couldn't get up. He felt he was sinking deeper and deeper into the couch with each passing second. His feet were swollen from being on them all night, his legs felt like jelly; he propped them up on the coffee table to get a little relief. He'd just close his eyes for a minute until Winnie came back from wherever she'd gone. Maybe she was falling asleep, too . . .

DANIEL WOKE UNHAPPILY to the slamming of a door. He lifted a hand to rub his face and found that his arms had been covered with a soft plaid wool blanket that he didn't recognize. It was white with silver running in a thin pattern. Pendleton wool, pricey. Winnie must have covered him up; her nachos had disappeared from the counter.

"Oh crap," Ainsley groaned, dropping her stuff onto a bar stool. It didn't stay and fell to the floor with a thud that made Daniel glad he didn't live below her. "We were going to build that thing today, weren't we? I *knew* I was forgetting something . . ."

"It's okay." He'd apparently slumped over, resting his head on the arm of the couch, and he sat up, looking around. There was a hot-pink sticky note on the coffee table, and he worked to decipher the handwriting:

You fell asleep. Knock on my bedroom door when you want to go home, and I'll take you.

–Winnie

The thoughtful gesture brought a huge smile to his face; that was so her. She might put on a cold front at times, but deep down, he was starting to see that she was a generous friend. He loved that.

Ainsley plopped down next to him on the couch. "You know, it would help me remember if you were actually mad at me when I forgot our hang-outs."

"No, it wouldn't," he said, tipping over to put his head on her shoulder. He yawned again, pulling the blanket up higher over himself. "Besides, it's part of your charm."

"Don't go to sleep on me," she said, pushing at his shoulder. "I've got stuff to do."

She stood up, and without her supporting him, he tipped over to lie flat against the couch cushions. "Harumpsh."

Ainsley snickered. "What does that mean?" she asked, as she unloaded the dishwasher.

"That's the noise tired doctors make when they sleep in a weird position all day waiting for their inconsiderate friend to come home." Daniel sat up again, rubbing at his sore neck with both hands. Winnie appeared in the entrance to the living room looking bleary-eyed, a fuzzy rose shawl around her shoulders. The woman had a thing for pink. "Ainsley wake you up, too?"

She nodded, rubbing her eyes.

"You guys want dinner?"

"No, I've got dinner with my grandparents today."

"Oh, that's right. I knew that. Daniel, you hungry?"

There was a knock at the front door, and Winnie went to answer it, yawning.

"Mom?"

"Hello, Winifred."

Daniel sat upright immediately at the sound of his mentor's voice, as if someone had thrown a lever and ejected him from the couch. Dr. Baker was leaning away from the kiss on the cheek she'd given her daughter, staring at him, her features tight. "Dr. Durand?"

"Dr. Baker, nice to see you."

Her piercing gaze bounced between the blanket, Winnie's pajama-ed appearance, and his own disheveled clothing. She didn't need to say anything for him to read the assumptions she was making and the stark displeasure she felt about them.

"I was just visiting my friend, Ainsley Buchanan. Have you two met?"

"Yes, we have." Her voice was flat. "Hello, Ainsley. Winifred, are you ready to go?"

"I'm sorry, I didn't realize you were picking me up. Back in a flash."

"Please hurry. You know they don't like it when we're late."

"Yes, I'll . . ." She walked briskly toward the hallway. "I'll be right there," she called back over her shoulder as she disappeared into the darkness.

With Winnie gone, Dr. Baker's attention turned back to Daniel. "How was your shift yesterday evening?"

"It was fine, thank you."

"Are you getting your study hours in?" She made no move to come closer, her hands folded in front of her, her body motionless. "This is a new program. I would hate to see it fail for lack of ambition on the part of the participants."

"Yes, I'm just . . . I was just . . ." *Why is it that every time we talk she makes me feel like a toddler who didn't make it to the toilet?*

Winnie entered the living room, still putting on her pearl post earrings, her navy-blue ballet flats tucked under her arm and a red cardigan over her shoulders. "Ready?"

"When you are," Dr. Baker replied, still keeping her gaze trained on Daniel. He rose from the couch and strolled toward the front door, running a hand over his bound hair. He wanted to say something to Winnie, to respond to the note she'd left, the way she'd tucked him in.

"Thanks for the ride and for breakfast, Fred." He winced internally as Dr. Baker's spine somehow went even straighter, and she looked at her daughter critically. Winnie looked at him in shock, staring at him so long, he was nervous that she was having some sort of episode. "What?"

"My dad called me Fred. He was the only one."

"Should I not . . . ," he started, but she shook her head.

"No, it's okay." Winnie just gave him a small smile as she put on her puffy white winter coat. "And you're welcome. I enjoyed it."

"Winifred. Let's go." Dr. Baker herded Winnie out the door, then turned to Daniel, her voice low enough that her daughter wouldn't hear. "Don't lose your focus, Dr. Durand. It wouldn't pay to get distracted at this stage of your career."

She shut the door quietly behind them, and Daniel turned to Ainsley, his eyes wide.

"Did she just tell me to stay away from her daughter?"

Ainsley nodded as she measured cornmeal into her batter bowl. "I believe she did, yes."

He put his hands on his hips and stared at the closed door. "Well, that's not going to happen."

She grinned. "I thought you might say that. You're staying for chili, right? Don't go to Subway again. I know that's what you were planning. Man cannot live on takeout alone."

"Fine, I'll stay." Daniel laughed sheepishly, then shuffled over to try to make heads or tails of the pile of lumber stacked in their living room.

CHAPTER TEN

"DID YOU GET THE DATE you wanted for the MCATs?"

The question shouldn't have surprised her: being trapped together in the car was the perfect time for her mother to try to squeeze information out of her. Sandra continued without waiting for an answer.

"From what I can tell, the latest testing date you'd want is April twenty-fifth; the results come back May twenty-seventh, and then admissions open up June first . . ."

"I haven't signed up yet."

"Do you need money?"

Winnie actively suppressed an eye roll. Her mother was convinced that midwifery didn't pay nearly enough and would eventually have Winnie begging under the Burnside Bridge.

"No, I have money."

"Then what's the barrier? I thought you were going to lock down your date weeks ago. I can set aside some time to help you study, but I'd like to get it on the calendar now."

Yes, thought Winnie, *because all that solitary wine drinking and literary fiction reading can't be rearranged at a moment's notice.* "I'll let you know when I've got my date."

"Just don't put it off too long or it'll be too late."

Winnie waited a few moments before changing the subject. "Speaking of dates, how was your dinner with the dermatologist?"

Her mother shook her head a little. "Uncomfortable."

"Oh, I'm sorry. Why?"

"He wasn't a good conversationalist. There were these stilted lapses in our discussions, no matter what topic I selected. I was obligated to carry most of it myself. I never had that problem with your father."

Winnie smiled a little. When her mother recounted her tales of dating woe, they often ended like this, comparing all the ways the other man wasn't Kent. Admittedly, her father had been an excellent companion when it came to stimulating conversation. Winnie herself had often looked down to find her food stone cold at the dinner table, because she'd been so enraptured as he recounted his day and what his classes had discussed. People who thought literature boring had obviously never taken a class from Dr. Kent Baker.

At the same time, Winnie thought, it probably wasn't healthy to still be comparing every new man to him two decades later. It was hard to imagine her mother married again, but she didn't like to think of her being lonely, either.

"Maybe you just need to develop some common interests with someone first. Join a book club or something..."

"You know I don't have the margin in my personal life for such things. My work must come before everything else. You'll understand someday."

This again. Somehow, like a carousel, they always circled around to the same topic. Winnie was definitely ready to get off the ride. She might throw up otherwise.

Dinner was seafood paella this week, complete with roasted peppers, salad, fresh bread, and fried plantains.

"Grandma, this is amazing," Winnie said, taking a second helping of the paella, ignoring the dirty look her mother was giving her. She was no doubt judging how many carbs Winnie was putting into her body. But this was by far the best food she'd eaten all week, and she deserved to enjoy it. She'd just closed her eyes to savor her next bite in the peaceful darkness of her own judgment-free zone when her grandfather spoke.

"Read any good books lately, Winnie?" Howard asked.

She nodded. "It's called *The Arrival* by Shaun Tan. I checked it out from the library; my friend Starla recommended it." She did not mention that she only acted on the advice because of Daniel's influence. "It depicts the immigrant experience in a fantasy setting. I intended to just page through it briefly before bed, but I ended up staying up well past midnight to finish it."

"It's a novel?" her mother asked.

"No. Well, yes, it's a *graphic* novel. Wordless, no less. But it was extremely moving, and the artwork was just spectacular."

Sandra's silence and high eyebrows spoke volumes as she helped herself to another large glass of wine; she wouldn't bother debating the merits of a book with pictures, never mind that all of Winnie's favorite books favored that medium. She'd been told plenty of times that "real books" didn't need them. She simply disagreed.

"How about you, Grandpa? What are you reading?"

"Just finished another Dortmunder. That guy's gotta be the worst criminal in the world."

Winnie grinned. "How many of those are there, anyway?"

"Plenty. Come sit with me while I smoke, won't you?"

"Sure, Grandpa." The covered porch in the back was quiet at this time of night except for the occasional semi-truck lumbering by on Highway 226. She'd always liked their yard. It backed right up to the woods, a natural wildness infecting her grandmother's attempts to have an orderly property. Howard turned on the gas patio heater for her, and she curled up on a wicker chair that had a quilt patterned after the American flag on it.

"Your grandma tells me you're taking the MCATs again."

"That's the plan."

He nodded slowly as he lit his cigar and took a long drag. "You know, your dad thought about studying dentistry."

Winnie reared back. "What? Really?"

"Honest to God. He even went so far as to take organic chemistry."

"Wow. How'd that go?"

"Oh"—he chuckled—"about like you'd expect. Kent tried his darndest to make it work, but I think the only reason he wanted to be a dentist was so he could tell people stories without being interrupted. Then he figured out that he could do the same thing if they were paying to listen to him teach."

"He was a good teacher."

"A good writer, too. But that stopped when he met your mom."

"Really? Why?"

"Never asked him. I assumed once you came along, he didn't have as much time." He blew the smoke away from Winnie, but the breeze carried it back. Rain pattered steadily against the leaf-littered ground where the yard met the woods.

The security light that had come on when they walked out turned off again, and they were left sitting in a comfortable darkness.

"I miss him."

"So do I. No offense to you ladies, but Kent was a lot more interested in hunting than you three are."

"I prefer to bring life into the world than take it out, thank you very much."

"You wouldn't miss helping with births? Counseling women?"

Winnie shifted to pull her knees into her chest. "I could focus on obstetrics and gynecology."

"I'm just a dumb economics professor, but that doesn't seem to have the same vibe as your current workplace activities."

She said nothing, picking at a dry spot on her skin.

Howard sighed. "I just want to see you examine this choice from all angles, kiddo. That's all. I'm here if you want to talk it over."

"Okay. Thank you."

"How's the boyfriend? What's his name?"

"Daniel?" She wanted to slap a hand over her mouth. Why had she said that?

"No, it started with *E* . . . Evan? Ellsworth?"

She laughed. "Ethan. He's long gone, Grandpa."

"Just as well. I didn't buy his schmooze act the one time he came over." He put out his cigar. "But now that we're on the subject, who's Daniel?"

Winnie felt her cheeks heat. "No one. One of Mom's protégés. We talked about him last week, remember?"

"Yeah, but why would you bring him up in the boyfriend context?"

"He . . . he likes me, I think." It seemed politer than "he's obviously very infatuated with me." That would come off as prideful.

"Smart boy."

"He's too young for me, though. He'd be in it for the short term, and I don't have any interest in that. Still kind of a kid at heart." *Which I shouldn't like about him, but . . .*

"He's legal, isn't he?"

She rolled her eyes. "Yes, Grandpa. It'd be tough to be in residency if you weren't eighteen. I think he's twenty-four."

"Aw, that's nothing. Plus, he can fix our universal remote when the batteries fall out."

"He's actually really bad with technology. I had to show him how to take his phone off 'do not disturb' the other day."

"Always finding little reasons to talk to you, is he?"

Winnie blinked. Was he? Now that she thought about it, it didn't make sense at all that he didn't know how to do that.

"We're just friends. I'm sure Dr. Baker wouldn't approve."

"She's good at disapproving. Don't let it get to you, honey."

Tears unexpectedly sprang to Winnie's eyes. "I'll try," she whispered.

CHAPTER
ELEVEN

THE NEXT DAY WAS ODDLY slow. She was supposed to have two appointments this morning, but they both canceled. Without overthinking it, she wandered into family medicine and took in the stack of work to be done. Yes, she was a mid-wife, but she was also still a nurse. She could give them a hand if she had time.

"What are you doing still here?" Martina asked, claiming a rolling chair.

"Just wanted to give you a hand."

"We're short because of the Ralston wedding, the one in town. Everyone wanted time off, no one made sure we were covered . . ."

Winnie sighed. "That reminds me, I still need a date to that wedding."

"Your professor's?"

She nodded. "I really should go. And I do want to, I just . . ."

"Need arm candy first."

"Exactly. I mean, I could take my cousin, probably."

"*Do not* take your cousin. I mean it, Winnie. It's a no go."

"Hey!" Daniel's voice made her spin around. "What are you up to?"

"Nothing yet. You?"

"Just finished a well-child visit. He's gonna need shots. I hate giving little kids shots."

Winnie blinked at him. Doctors didn't give shots. Doctors had more important things to do. "Why would you give his shots?"

"Your mom insists it's good experience. Plus, everybody's crazy busy today. I can do it. I just don't like it."

Winnie peeked at the chart he was holding and winced. "He's five? Those are the worst. They know what's coming."

"Like cows who won't get in the chute."

"Pardon?"

"Never mind. Farm analogy."

Winnie put one hand on her hip. "Did you grow up on a farm? You don't wear enough John Deere or Dickies clothing for that."

"No, but my classmates did. And they assured me that some cows know when it's slaughter time. Cows that don't mind lining up on any old Monday are digging in their hooves on Friday."

"Are cows slaughtered on a Friday?"

He slapped down the chart in faux exasperation. "I don't know, Fred, I make things up, okay? It's funnier that way." He turned to face her. "Will you help me distract him? It's better with two people." Was he . . . ? Yes, he was. Daniel Durand was giving her the doe eyes like a darn Disney prince, and those eyelashes totally worked for him.

"You're pathetic. Who are you sticking?"

"Jackson Vallens."

She didn't even try to stop the way her heart went Technicolor. "Oh, I was there when he was born at OHSU. He was one of my first deliveries."

Daniel flicked his wrist forward, pantomiming casting a fishing line, hooking Winnie and reeling in slowly.

She rolled her eyes, but his antics did make her and Martina laugh. "Fine. I'll help you, but just for a minute, and only because I'd very much enjoy seeing Kelly and Jackson again."

"Nurse Baker, you're my hero."

"Yeah, yeah."

Martina was giving her heart eyes and making a kissing face, but thankfully, he didn't notice as he led the way to Jackson's room and knocked. Kelly's smooth, even voice paused, momentarily abandoning the book they were reading, to call, "Come in."

Jackson's anxiety was obvious as he clutched a shaggy brown bear with a red ribbon around its neck, sitting on his mom's lap.

"Hi, Mrs. Vallens, hi, Jackson. I'm Dr. Durand. Sorry for the wait," Daniel said, "we're short-staffed today. Lots of people out sick with the flu." Most doctors only greeted the parents; he'd greeted Jackson as well, she noticed.

"It's been awful this year, hasn't it?" Kelly commented. A smile split her face when she saw Winnie. "Well, hello, stranger! How've you been? Jackson, say hi to Miss Winnie, she was there when you were born."

Jackson mumbled a greeting as his mother shifted him off her lap to give Winnie a one-armed hug.

"Small world, isn't it?" Winnie smiled, returning her hug. "It's great to see you." She turned her attention back to Daniel, who was giving her a meaningful look she couldn't interpret. He tipped his head toward the waiting tray, and she rolled her eyes. Apparently, being the nurse in the room meant it was *her* job to prep everything. Sigh. She pulled out the alcohol wipes as Daniel chatted with the boy about the book they'd interrupted: *Llama Llama Mad at Mama. Yes,* Winnie chuckled inwardly, *he will probably be mad at you after this.* They only had two shots to do, a DPT booster with varicella and a flu shot. They could each take a side and get it over twice as quickly . . .

"Jackson, do you sleep on your side or on your back?" Daniel asked, sitting in the rolling chair and pulling himself over to the boy with his heels.

"On my side," he said, rubbing his arm, as if trying to protect it from the mean old doctor.

"Which one?" Daniel asked. "Because I want to put your shots in the other arm so you can sleep really good tonight, okay? Can you show me which arm is against the bed?"

Jackson's eyebrows dipped as he considered this, then lifted his left arm.

"Is that right, Mom?" Daniel asked, and Kelly shrugged.

"I think so, but honestly, I never noticed."

"That's okay, we'll take his word for it," Daniel said. "Nurse Baker, would you come on this side for me? Mom, can you sit on the exam table with Jackson on your lap?" They scooted and slid past each other, the exam room feeling smaller than it really was, until they'd reordered themselves as he'd requested. When everyone had settled into place, Daniel stood in front of Jackson, his legs braced open wide. This was a prime kicking moment, but somehow, he wasn't sensing the danger this posed to some very sensitive parts of his body, and he continued to swab a wide swatch of Jackson's arm, oblivious. Winnie bit the inside of her lip. Should she say something? If he got kicked in the crotch, she'd feel responsible. Yes, it was his crotch, but she'd have seen it coming. It was like not telling a friend when they had spinach in their teeth, only a hundred times worse. But she didn't want him thinking that she was thinking about his crotch—except she kind of was. But in a friendly way, not in a sexy way.

"Wait," she blurted. "Kelly, cross your legs over Jackson's legs, would you? Just in case."

Kelly looked perplexed, but did so, holding her son's arms and legs still. The caps came off, the needles went in, and just as Winnie had predicted, Jackson bucked and squirmed, shouting his displeasure, his thrashing foot still catching Daniel in the knee.

"I'm so sorry," Kelly said, obviously chagrined, as Daniel rubbed his leg.

"No worries. War wounds are part of the job," he joked. Yet it was obvious by the tension around his mouth, despite his forced smile, that Jackson had landed his blow in the same spot as Daniel's cycling injury. It was going to hurt tomorrow, too. Maybe he'd like some of her helichrysum rub . . . Wait, no. That would be inappropriately forward. He could take care of himself. But as she watched him pretend his leg didn't smart like the dickens, a surge of tenderness toward the man rose within her; she felt a stomachache forming, hating his pain as much as if it were her own. Surprised at herself, she left Daniel to finish up with Kelly as he reminded her to watch for signs of a bad reaction. Across the hall, she ducked into the supply room, her heart beating fast. It wouldn't take long for him to be called away, distracted. But when she heard the door quietly open and snick shut behind her, Winnie knew she was caught.

"Hiding again, Fred?"

"And why would I do that?" She tried valiantly to keep her voice steady, but when she felt his heat behind her, she knew she'd failed.

"You knew how he was going to react. You tried to save me, Winnie Baker."

She rearranged several bottles of isopropyl alcohol that were already stored very neatly. "It's called professional courtesy."

"Yes, thinking about how to prevent my genitals from getting kicked is a very professional line of thinking."

Despite having her back to him, she lifted her chin defiantly. "Wouldn't you do the same for me?"

"Oh, Winnie," he murmured. "You've no idea what I'd do for you, if you asked me to. I just wanted you to know you don't have to try and hide how good your heart is; it's obvious. Your thoughtfulness touches everyone around you, including me." She wished she could see his face. Then she'd know if this was just a line or sincerity . . . It *felt* like sincerity. His knuckles skirted over her upper arm, but when she didn't react, the touch disappeared. She was still trying to recover from shock when he silently slipped out of the closet, closing the door behind him.

CHAPTER
TWELVE

THE NEXT DAY, WINNIE sat down at her desk in the nurses' station. Without meaning to, she glanced up at the clock—1:52. *Perfect timing.* When she looked down, there was a cylindrical white box on the desk the size of a soft drink. Someone had attached a printed label to it that said, "Winnie Baker, open me." She glanced around, but everyone seemed preoccupied by their own responsibilities. Furtively, she cracked the lid, and what she saw made her grin: A Thor bobblehead, holding his tiny hammer. On a hot-pink sticky note fixed to the inside of the lid, Daniel had somehow printed out a typed message:

Thank you for your heroic protection the other day. You're welcome in Asgard anytime. Hope this guy can make you smile when I'm not around.

–D

Right on schedule a few minutes later, Daniel Durand came wandering down the hallway and leaned on the counter. "Did you get my present?"

"I did."

"Did you like it?"

"He doesn't have your sense of style, but I suppose he's a suitable stand-in. He's certainly as hardheaded as you."

Daniel didn't respond, and she looked up to find him staring at her, his gaze soft. Those long eyelashes, his blond stubble, the faint scent of cinnamon that seemed to follow him had her grinning . . . *I shouldn't be encouraging this.* The reasons why were escaping her when faced with his pretty eyes. *Young? Right, young. Plus, he'd probably be out of here the minute he found out what a liar I am.* Chiding herself, she broke away from the moment, putting her eyes back on her paperwork.

"Fred, are you familiar with the Egyptian plover?"

She raised an eyebrow without looking up, then went back to her paperwork without answering. *Must avoid pretty eyes. Avoid! Avoid!*

"My grandma, you see," he continued, "she was crazy about birds, so she was always making us read about them and go birding. But that was lame, because my favorite bird was the Egyptian plover, which, of course, is rarely seen in Oregon."

"I'd be willing to bet it's never seen in Oregon."

"Smart lady." He grinned. "Do you want to know why it's my favorite?"

"Not really," she said, but she knew he saw the corner of her mouth flexing as she fought a smile.

"There's no modern corroboration, but they say Egyptian plovers will find crocodiles with their mouths open and hop in there to grab a quick meal of the meat between their teeth."

Winnie set down her pen and folded her hands in her lap. "What are you trying to say, Dr. Durand?"

"I'm saying don't bite my head off, and maybe I'll go with you to that thing."

"Thing? What thing?"

He gestured vaguely in the air between them. "The wedding thing. I heard you talking to Martina." She gave him her full attention. He certainly fit the part that she was looking for: arm candy. Successful, charming arm candy to parade around in front of Ethan. But she barely knew Daniel. She should just take her cousin Harrison. Yes, Ethan would know who he was, but no one else would.

"Eavesdropping is a terrible habit."

"Can't argue with you, but the point remains that there's potential mutual benefit here, croc." She didn't mind being the predator in the analogy, but something was still missing. He was far too young to truly be interested in her for more than just a fling.

"What's in it for you?" she asked.

"Pardon?"

"Well, to use your analogy, the plover's getting a meal. What are you getting?"

"Besides the pleasure of your company for an evening? I had assumed there would be food at this thing . . . Is there not food? If there's no food, I'm out."

Her furrowed expression just deepened. "You're serious?"

"As late-stage pancreatic cancer."

"That's a very insensitive simile."

"I love a woman who knows her literary devices." He grinned. "Come on, it'll be fun. I'm a good dancer. I won't get drunk and embarrass you. I look great in a tux, and I already own one." He threw out his arms as he backed away from the station slowly and turned, as if showing himself off. He needn't have bothered; she'd spent a fair amount of time cataloguing his best features already. Not that she would ever admit that unless under pain of death.

"Just think about it," he said, then he hurried down the hall to catch up with his residency group, who were already gathering for their lecture.

And to her surprise, she was. She was thinking about it, even if Bobblehead Thor was shaking his head at her.

"HAVE YOU THOUGHT ABOUT my offer?" Daniel leaned over the nurses' station a few days later, tapping Thor's head to make it wobble. He was finding it hard to be patient, waiting for her verdict to come down. He wanted to dance with her, drink with her . . . He'd probably stick to Sprite, but still. Their interaction in the closet was still fresh in his mind; he thought maybe he'd backed off too quickly. Or maybe he'd come on too strong? He didn't know how to do slow, and it was messing with his mojo.

"Yes," Winnie replied, and his heart leaped until she continued. "But I think our age difference could pose a problem. I don't want people commenting on it."

"Age is just a state of mind."

"Spoken like someone young."

"Oh, come on. You're acting like you're Father Time and I'm the New Year's baby."

"Having as much experience with babies as I do, you'll forgive me if I can't help but note the similarities."

Daniel leaned forward on his elbows, resting his chin in his hand. "Oh, really? Is it my soft skin? Do I smell like powder? Do tell."

Her cheeks went pink. "You're ridiculous."

"Me?" He laughed. "You're the one who won't give me the time of day just because we were born in slightly different decades."

"Yes," she said, slapping her charts down onto the counter, "different *decades*. I'm so much older than you, I'm surprised I can even understand what you're saying."

Goading her was too easy, not to mention fun.

"Spill the tea, girl." He grinned. "Am I too basic for you?"

"Ugh." Winnie turned and headed back toward the elevators.

No, don't run off like that . . .

"Damn, Gina! Why you gotta be so salty?" he called after her.

"Dr. Durand." At the cold sound of Dr. Baker's voice, Daniel spun, chagrined. "There are patients attempting to recuperate nearby. Please lower your voice to a decent volume."

He shoved his hands deep into his coat. "I apologize, Dr. Baker."

She sauntered closer, and he recognized the move as one that Winnie shared. It reminded him of a lioness stalking her prey.

"I notice you're spending more time socializing with my daughter lately."

He didn't want to lie, but a creeping sense of foreboding stole over him. "Oh yeah?"

"Yeah," she said, drawing out the word to make perfectly clear how she disdained his diction. "And her name is Winifred, not Gina."

"Oh, yes, ma'am, I know her name, that phrase means . . . it means something else." Her skeptical glare did make him feel like the New Year's baby. "It's a TV reference," he said, resisting the urge to flee.

"Is it?" It didn't sound like a question, really, so he stayed quiet. When it came to Dr. Baker, he really thought his best bet was just not talking unless called upon to do so. When Dr. Trout distracted her, Daniel slipped away.

CHAPTER THIRTEEN

IT WAS 11:30 A.M. WINNIE had been called in to assist with a difficult birth early that morning, and she wasn't watching where she was going. She'd been kicked, pinched, scratched and screamed at already today, and she was done. Outside the locker rooms, she ran into Daniel.

"Geez, you can't swing a stethoscope around here without hitting a hospital employee named Durand."

"Small-town hazard." He grinned. "Are you going to have lunch with your mom before you go?"

She felt her expression shutter. "No. She's already found a lunch date."

"Who, Dr. Udawatte? I'm sure you could join them."

She patted his chest. "It's nice that you think you're being nice."

He wasn't scowling, exactly, but he looked perplexed. "Seriously, Tharushi's super nice."

"I'm sure she is. But I'm going to head home."

He took her hand and began to drag her across the cafeteria. "Come on, I'll introduce you."

Winnie planted her feet and pulled her hand out of his grasp. "We've met." And she did not have the energy right now to make small talk with her mother's new protégée.

"You don't like her?" He looked astonished. "Why?"

She noticed several other people around them now tuned into their conversation, some more subtly than others, and she certainly didn't want to come off looking like a racist. "I like Dr. Udawatte. She's great, I just . . . I need to get home. I haven't slept."

"Okay." Winnie knew he wanted more information, but apparently, he was reading her well enough to see that he wasn't going to get it now. She turned on the heel of her flats and headed for the front exit.

"You're going to Rico's, aren't you? Don't deny it."

She shook her head, pursing her lips to keep a smile off them. "I had thought of it," she admitted, "but I should probably eat a salad or something."

"That's what a good doctor would tell you to do," he said, as he came level with her, matching her stride. "I, on the other hand, maintain the importance of daily pico de gallo."

"Winnie?"

A familiar voice had her shoulders tensing even before she saw his face. At this point, just thinking about him could bring on a headache. He wore his usual work clothes—a white button-down with gray slacks under a blue windbreaker—and leaned against one of the cement columns of the portico like he'd been waiting for her.

"Ethan? What are you doing here?"

He stood up straight and began to come closer. "You didn't return my messages . . ."

"Yes, there's a—" She started to remind him that there was a reason for that, a very good one. But she didn't want to do this with Daniel standing right there, who had taken on a look of pointed curiosity. "Would you please excuse us, Dr. Durand?"

His light scowl and the deep lines around his mouth told her this was not what Daniel was expecting, but he nodded slowly. "I'll just be inside if you need me."

"Okay, thank you."

He stood there for another long moment, giving Ethan an unfriendly stare before heading in.

Winnie turned back to Ethan, keeping her voice low and even. "You and I are not together anymore. I don't want to have lunch with you."

"Are you dating him?" Ethan asked, jerking his head toward Daniel's back.

"If I am, it's none of your business. I am none of your business. I would like you to leave."

"Winnie," he said with a desperate edge to his voice, "I made a mistake, all right? I should never have broken up with you. I miss you so much."

She lifted her chin. "I'm sorry to hear that. I suggest that you find a qualified mental health professional with whom you can discuss your troubles."

"Are you going to Dr. Weaver's wedding? We should go together." He stepped closer, reaching out to stroke her arm, finding her fingers and intertwining them with his. "Please, Win. It'll give us a chance to talk. We can overcome our differences, I know we can."

Winnie looked around, desperately hoping someone would come by who could distract from this unwanted attention. But the only presence in the parking lot was the wind, gusting hard enough to make the wind chimes in the memorial cancer garden audible, even from this distance. She wanted to pull away, but not enough to cause a scene; someone could come outside at any moment . . . If she'd just let Daniel stay, Ethan might not have been so forward. *Why did I send him inside? My stupid pride? Either way, there's no one here now,* she argued with herself. *It wouldn't be a scene. Just tell him not to touch you. Make him leave you alone.* But Winnie just stared down at their linked hands, fighting to breathe normally.

"Yes, I'm going, but I already have a date." A lie she would make true at the first opportunity.

He withdrew his hand slowly. "I see."

Winnie looked up at him, and the pain in his face felt like a sucker punch, even though she thought she didn't care.

"You'll save a dance for me, though, won't you?" The wind blasted them again, and Ethan tucked a piece of her wind-tossed hair behind her ear. "I want another chance, Win. This guy can't love you like I can."

She looked away, not knowing what to say in lieu of the truth: *I'd rather run naked up and down the aisle during the whole ceremony than let you touch me again, even once. You hurt me, left me. We're done.* Why wasn't he getting the message here? Was she somehow being unclear? Had he always been so delusional? He hadn't talked much about his other exes when they were dating, something she'd liked about him at the time; were they avoiding him because he was badgering them? Staring into his blue eyes now, she wondered what she'd seen in him at all.

"I'll see you at the wedding, I guess," she said, stepping around him, pivoting so she didn't have to put her back to him.

"I look forward to it," he said, giving her one of the smiles that used to make her knees weak. Now it just made her temples pulse painfully. She turned and hurried to her car before he could say anything else, her hands shaking as she pulled out her keys. She sat behind the steering wheel, angry, watching him get into his silver Rover.

CHAPTER
FOURTEEN

DANIEL STOOD AT THE sliding glass doors of the hospital, watching Winnie talk with the man she'd identified as Ethan. This must be the boyfriend who wasn't getting the message. And boy, was he not getting the message: every time Ethan touched Winnie, Daniel could see the discomfort radiating from her like he was watching her on an infrared camera, layer upon layer of heat encircling her. It was taking all his self-control not to call security and have the man escorted from the property for harassing the staff . . . But Winnie had asked him to leave them alone. He couldn't start disregarding her wishes; he would listen to what she wanted, unlike this schmuck. So he stood, fists shoved deep into his pockets, just watching. Daniel was debating what he would do if Ethan tried to kiss her when he felt someone amble up next to him.

"What are we doing?" Kyle asked. "Who is that?"

"Winnie's ex. Ethan."

Kyle adopted a similar posture. "I don't like him."

That did make Daniel's face crack into a small smile. "You've never even met him."

"Look at his shoes. They're all shiny and pretentious." Kyle was silent for a moment. "I don't need to meet him. Look at

Winnie, she's clearly uncomfortable. That's enough information for me." He turned toward Daniel to see him better. "Are
you going to let him treat her like that?" Kyle pushed up his
sleeves. "Let me go talk to him. You're not intimidating; you
have that baby face thing happening."

"No," Daniel said, putting a hand on his brother's arm.
Kyle's lack of social graces was going to get him into real trouble someday; not everyone was willing to overlook them as a
by-product of his autism. "He's leaving, anyway." *Good.* Daniel
watched her long enough to make sure she got to her car all
right, then turned to his brother. "We have no say in the matter,
and it's not our business. She asked me to go inside. I'm sure she
can handle it."

"Then why were we still standing here?"

"In case I was wrong."

Kyle nodded. "Yeah, you're wrong a lot."

Daniel rolled his eyes. "Thank you, that's very encouraging." *Ten bucks says the sarcasm goes right over his head . . .*

"You're welcome." He glanced out the window. "Also, here
she comes."

The doors opened and Winnie blasted into the building,
her hair windblown and her cheeks flushed. Everything in him
wanted to hurry over to her, ask if she was okay, but he made
himself stand still as she came to him, glancing at Kyle.

"I have thought about your offer."

Music to my ears. "And?"

"And I would like for you to escort me, if you're still willing."

*Jackpot. Also, her sprinting away from her ex in order to se-
cure me as her date? Totally fine with that.*

He grinned. "Ready, willing, and able. Just tell me where and when."

"The wedding is at five at the Benson Hotel in downtown Portland, Saturday after next."

"Swanky," commented Kyle. "Our uncle Buster got married there."

"Oh?"

"Yeah. All four times," Daniel said.

Winnie rolled her eyes. "Give me your address, and I'll pick you up at two."

"No way. This is a date—our *first* date. I'm a gentleman. A gentleman always picks up his lady, lest she have to pay for gas." When she hesitated, he smiled. "Also, we'll get there faster if I drive."

"Fine. But only because I hate driving in heels. Do not"—she pointed at him—"be late. In fact, let's make it 1:45."

"That's hurtful, Fred. Your friendly neighborhood escort would not do that to you. I'm a very prompt individual. Everyone knows if you're not five minutes early, you're late. Just in case, I'll need your phone number."

"971-235-"

"You know, on second thought, can you just text it to me? Here's mine." He turned his phone so she could see it. *Because missing our date due to my dyslexic brain putting your number in wrong would be a true tragedy.* Pushing the thought aside, he bounced his eyebrows. "Are we staying the night?"

"Yes—in separate rooms. We're invited to brunch on Sunday, then we'll drive back."

He couldn't keep the smile off his face; he wasn't surprised he was getting his own room, and frankly, he didn't care. *I'm going on a fancy date with Winnie Baker.*

"This is going to be fun. I'm excited. Are you excited? I like wearing my tux. I hardly ever get the chance."

"You could always chaperone for prom."

He scowled at her disdainfully. "That's one night, Fred. That doesn't serve my needs at all . . . I'm glad you decided to take me up on my offer. It's a favor to me, really."

She was smiling as she exited the building again, hopefully to actually go home this time.

What a great day.

WHAT A CRAPPY DAY.

"This makes no sense," Daniel mumbled to himself a few hours later, paging through Norm Horowitz's chart. He'd been on an IV since noon, but based on his sunken eyes and lack of trips to the bathroom, it wasn't working. Daniel got the sphygmomanometer off the wall and took his blood pressure. His wife, Sarai, sat on his other side, rubbing his arm, holding his hand, pulling the bleached covers up at intervals.

"Our son Ryan's an EMT, and he recommended we come in," she explained unnecessarily. "Norm's been vomiting."

"I'm glad you did, the flu's been going around," Daniel said, trying to focus on taking the reading—90/56. Too low still. He sighed as he turned to the computer to update the stats. It was the same as it had been when he checked it at two . . . What was going on? Daniel pulled out his phone to page Dr. Baker, but bobbled it and dropped it with a clatter against the white tile. Norm stirred, and Sarai glared at Daniel in annoyance for bothering him.

"Sorry," he muttered as he bent to retrieve it . . . which is when he noticed the front right wheel of the hospital bed, sitting on Mr. Horowitz's IV wide-open tube. He wanted to sigh; a small hospital meant older technology and no alarm to notify them that the line was occluded. Regardless of whose fault it was, he didn't want to expose them; it could've easily been his mistake on another day. He knocked his shoulder hard against the bed, and the pinched tube popped free as the wheels rocked. He touched the plastic, making sure it hadn't cracked or broken, but it seemed fine. Daniel straightened and smiled down at a bewildered Mr. Horowitz. "Okay, sir, I think I've isolated the problem. I'd like to give this IV a little more time to work. I'll be back to check on you in a bit."

He ran into Kyle in the hallway.

"How's my patient?"

"Not recovering."

"Really?" Kyle frowned. "Why?"

"Someone rolled the bed onto the IV tube. I just fixed it."

Kyle glanced at the clock and cursed low under his breath. "He should've had two or three liters of fluids by now, and instead he's had none? I should go check on him."

Daniel laid a hand on his shoulder. "I told him I'd be back soon. Give it a little time. I had to wake him to move the bed. He should sleep."

Kyle paused, looking between Daniel and the closed door, then sighed. "Okay. You're probably right." As he walked away, Daniel paged Dr. Baker out of caution, and she showed up a few minutes later.

"Let's go ahead and prescribe him an anti-diarrheal and an anti-emetic. Dr. Durand, you may do the honors." Daniel moved to sit in front of the computer, but her next words stopped him.

"Oh, the network is down. You'll have to just write it out." He felt the sweat beading on his forehead. He'd mostly been able to avoid this issue: text messages and online health management systems were very handy when your handwriting looked like a four-year-old's due to your learning disability. But there was no getting out of it . . .

Dr. Baker's gaze narrowed. "Is there a problem, Dr. Durand?"

"Nope. No. Let me just . . ." He found a prescription pad in the drawer and got out a pen. Painstakingly, he copied the patient's name and his onto the paper, then cross-referenced his other medications before choosing a generic for both. When he looked up, Dr. Baker was standing next to him, her hand out, palm up.

"I'll take it for you." Her voice was casual, almost friendly, but he knew he was about to get yelled at. It was the same feeling he'd had in school when the teacher passed back tests.

"Has anyone told you that your handwriting is uncommonly bad? Even for a doctor, it's nearly illegible."

"Yeah, it's not uncommon for people with dysgraphia, it's got a high comorbidity with dyslexia. Not usually a problem when the computers are working," he mumbled. "Would you excuse me?"

"Dr. Durand? Wait a moment, please."

Daniel pretended he hadn't heard her. He didn't trust himself to be respectful right now, and besides, she could be calling Kyle or their dad. Completely plausible in these busy hallways. And anyway, he couldn't risk making things worse with Dr. Baker on the very day her daughter had finally agreed to a date. That tender shoot of a relationship could so easily be crushed, and Dr. Baker's high heels were poised to do just that.

CHAPTER FIFTEEN

TWO WEEKS LATER, WINNIE stared at herself in the mirror. It was trendy, the contouring, the smoky eye, the shiny lipstick. She tugged at the strapless bra she wore under the off-the-shoulder black evening gown she'd borrowed from her mother. She didn't want to seem ungrateful; it was so nice of Martina and Ainsley to help her. It just . . . wasn't her. Her own reflection reminded her of a china doll her grandmother had given her years ago. She felt about as real. The doorbell rang.

"Shoot." There was no time to do anything about it now. She quickly put in her earrings.

"Winnie!"

"Coming!" she called from the bathroom, as she strapped on the shoes, wobbling a little on the carpet. She got the reaction she expected from her roommates when she stepped out into the living room.

"Ooh," they cooed and catcalled her, then babbled over each other about how glamorous and fantastic and incredible her transformation was.

Daniel smiled at her. "Ready to go?"

Ainsley smacked him with the back of her hand. "Obviously she's ready! Look how great she looks! Don't you think she looks great?"

Daniel paused, then shrugged. "Sure, yeah." That pause. That pause was telling.

Ainsley crossed her arms. "Don't mind him, Winnie. You look amazing."

Daniel reddened. "I mean . . . you look a little uncomfortable. You don't look like you *feel* great. That's all."

Winnie's mouth dropped open, and humiliation washed over her. Without a word, she turned and grabbed her purse and coat from the chair by the front door and went outside. He was smart enough to grab her suitcase on his way out.

"Fred?" Daniel's voice drifted down the stairway as he followed her. "Are you . . . okay? I'm sorry, I shouldn't have—"

"It's fine," she said, cutting him off. "Let's go." She was used to criticism, after all. She'd lived with the Criticism Queen herself all those years.

He opened the passenger side door for her, and she slid into the seat. The Volvo no longer smelled of stale french fries and spilled coffee; he'd even vacuumed it. They drove in silence for about twenty minutes, Daniel shooting her nervous looks, until finally it all came tumbling out of him in a rush.

"Look, I wasn't trying to hurt your feelings, Win. I was just surprised, that's all. You don't usually go in for all that high-maintenance stuff, so I've never seen you like this before."

"Well, it's not like I did it for you."

His voice was quiet. "Okay. Well." He cleared his throat. "You can plug in your phone if you want music, but the radio's busted."

"I'd prefer silence."

He pulled onto the shoulder, gravel making the tires skid a little as they came to a stop. "Winnie, look at me."

She kept her eyes on her hands in her lap, and he sighed.

"I just like your normal look, that's all I was saying. I like your haphazard ponytail and your teddy bear scrubs and your white tennis shoes and your light makeup, because you look . . . you look . . ." He swallowed. "You look like a baby-catching superhero, which is exactly what you are. I'm sorry I didn't make you feel beautiful when you came out, okay? Even though you look incredibly sexy right now, I guess I just prefer you in your natural state. You put all other women to shame on any given day."

She turned her head just enough to see him in her peripheral vision. "Really?"

"Really."

Well, knock me over with a feather. Daniel's eyes were serious for once, and the set of his jaw told her that the honesty hadn't been easy for him—and that he really was sorry he'd hurt her.

She paused. "Do you have any wet wipes?"

He gestured with a smile. "Check the glove box." All he had were rough brown restaurant napkins, but she used a little water from her water bottle and made it work. As he pulled back onto the highway, she carefully wiped her face. She didn't remove all of it, just some of the heaviness of it. Winnie considered her work in the visor's mirror, then turned to Daniel.

"Better?"

He nodded, glancing at her between attending to the road. "Better." The conversation turned, much to her relief, to books and movies and music and babies and pediatric illnesses and homeopathy. There was no bunny trail they wouldn't run down with vigor.

"How'd you get into comic books?" he asked, setting the cruise control as the traffic thinned out past Salem.

"My father liked them."

"That's bold for an English professor."

"I believe he took some flak for it around the department. But he was insistent that literature was literature. Once he was gone, it was a way to maintain my connection with who he'd been. That and crab. I love seafood, only because he did, too." She glanced at him, squeezing her phone. "What about you?"

He sat up a little straighter, keeping his gaze on the road. "I, uh, I struggled with reading as a kid. Dyslexia. Comic books were a little easier, they had more wordless context. Fewer speech tags. So my parents bought them by the box-load. My teachers had no idea that I'd read most of the classics they assigned as graphic novels."

Her respect for him skyrocketed. "How the heck did you do medical school with dyslexia? The reading must have been killer."

"Lots of things have audiobooks now, even textbooks. And my dad and my brother recorded some for me."

"Still. Daniel. That's insane."

He laughed. "Why? It has no bearing on my ability to diagnose or treat patients. Just my ability to learn. And I can work with it. Just another hurdle."

"Well, I'm impressed."

"Good." He winked at her. "Just wait until you see my dance moves." When he pulled into the hotel's underground parking garage, she was almost surprised at how distracted she'd been the whole journey. Daniel retrieved her bag despite her insistence that she could carry it herself.

"I don't want to be responsible for any more damage to Ainsley's hard work," he said, winking, as he dragged the heavy bag inside.

"Hello. There should be two rooms under Baker," she said to the clerk, distractedly digging around in her purse for her wallet.

"Yes. And I see you've been upgraded to a suite."

Winnie stopped moving. It was like she'd been sunk into concrete. "No. Not a suite. A suite is not two rooms." The clerk's sparkling smile faded to something far less comfortable. It probably had something to do with the ire in Winnie's gaze, which was now aimed directly at the poor young woman.

"I'm so sorry about the mix-up; the bride was trying to consolidate the rooms to accommodate some last-minute out-of-town guests . . ."

"It'll be fine, Win," Daniel murmured. "Don't worry about it."

"Fine?" she whispered back, her voice harsh. "How is this fine? How?"

He pivoted to the desk clerk. "Does it have two beds?"

She swallowed hard. "Yes, sir. It has a king in a private bedroom and a pull-out queen in the sofa."

"See?" he said, picking up their bags again. "Fine. Two of us, two beds. You can have the king. It'll be just fine."

"No," she said, raising her voice just enough to attract the notice of a few other guests who stood nearby. "I want what I had originally booked."

The clerk winced. "Since your rooms were technically booked in conjunction with the wedding, the bride had the discretion to change things around. I'm so sorry, but the hotel is completely booked. Again, Ms. Baker, I'm so sorry for the misunderstanding."

Fuming, Winnie slapped her credit card down on the counter, and the woman quickly ran it and gave it back, her look truly apologetic.

CHAPTER
SIXTEEN

WINNIE WAS WAITING for her Riesling at the bar when she spied Ethan. Daniel's gaze followed him across the paisley-carpeted ballroom, too, as Ethan wove his way between the tables laden with tall, gold-plated vases overflowing with greenery.

Daniel let his hand rest at her lower back, and she felt herself relax at the innocent gesture. "Wanna make out?"

"No, thank you."

"Just saying. It would send a clear message."

"So would a swift kick to the testicles, but I'm not going to do that, either. Let's just ignore him."

"Your call." He ordered a tonic and lime, and Winnie stared at his handsome profile as she sipped her wine.

"You can drink if you want. I don't mind."

"Nah, I'm good. This isn't about me."

"No reason not to enjoy yourself."

He turned to rest his elbows on the bar behind him, and she wondered if he wanted to keep an eye on Ethan, rather than turning his back to the room. "Well, maybe one reason . . ."

"If you're uncomfortable staying together, you can go home tonight. It's really okay."

He put his hand over hers where it rested on the marble bar. "Win. Quit worrying. It's fine. I'm fine. I just don't want to drink tonight." His gaze stayed on her, and it was just how she'd caught him staring at her during the ceremony. She couldn't quite read him, but the look was making her cheeks heat.

"It was a nice wedding, wasn't it?"

He nodded. "Will you dance with me?"

Her thoughts evaporated, but her gut reacted violently. *No. Not out of obligation. Not to put on a show.* "You don't have to pretend. It's fine, I don't—"

"You're right, I don't have to pretend. And I'm not."

"Why?" She didn't say it loud enough, and all her vulnerability leaked through.

"Maybe I like taking care of you. Maybe I like holding you. I've always been partial to the song 'Brown-Eyed Girl'; maybe it's a sign." He sipped his drink. "Or maybe I just don't want to re-enact that top-ten hit by Billy Idol in 1981."

She smiled so hard her face hurt. "You wouldn't be referring to 'Dancing with Myself,' would you?"

"See? I know old stuff." He held out his hand in offer, and she took it, but she pulled him over to their table, setting her wine down at her place. Daniel led her to the parquet dance floor. As they walked, she planned to play it high school style: straight zombie arms at his shoulders, keeping a healthy amount of distance between them.

But when he took her hand and placed it over his heart, clasping her fingers to his chest like they were precious, and looked in her eyes like *she* was precious, she lost all her resolve. She hooked her left arm around his shoulders as his right came around her waist and pulled her tight against him. Daniel swayed them gently.

He leaned forward to murmur in her ear. "See? It's not so bad, is it?"

"I never said it would be bad," she said softly. "I just don't want you to feel obligated . . ."

"I don't. Not one bit. I'd be lying if I said I hadn't been thinking about this moment all week."

She drew back a little to see into his eyes. "And how does the reality compare?"

"Even better." He leaned forward and brushed his nose against hers. The contact made the hairs on the back of her neck stand up, and she felt loose and warm like she'd just taken a long, hot bath.

"Can I cut in?" Ethan's voice was like standing up after the bath; a slap of cold air on her skin.

"No." Daniel was grinning, despite how he must have felt her tense up in his arms.

Ethan's eyes narrowed. "We haven't been properly introduced. I'm Ethan Pressbrook. And you are?"

"Dr. Daniel Durand," he said. "But as you can see, I'm too busy to shake your hand at the moment. Come find me later, and I'll see what I can do to you."

"For you," Winnie corrected, fighting a smile.

"Oops. For you. I'm sure I meant for you."

At her voice, Ethan turned his attention to her. "Man, Win. You clean up nice."

"The implication being that I usually look awful?" What was *in* that wine? Was it some kind of tasty truth serum? She was never so sassy on the outside.

He frowned. "No, I just meant—never mind. Look, I talked to your mom. Called your house, she said you'd moved. Said you were starting to grow up finally, taking the MCATs again. She asked me to give you another chance."

Daniel broke his hold on her and interlocked his fingers in a begging position. "Please let me get rid of this guy. Please, Fred. I won't break his nose."

"I beg your pardon?" Ethan asked, his voice hard. They both ignored him.

Her eyes narrowed. "What would you break?"

Daniel stroked his light beard in thought. "A thumb, maybe. Something that would be annoying, but not really terrible. I broke my thumb in first grade, just as I was learning to write. It was *no bueno*. This fool could use a taste of the discomfort he's causing you."

"*This fool?* I *just* introduced myself to you. Clearly you have the brain of a flea." Ethan never had liked being ignored.

"And who would know better than a dog?" Daniel returned with a smile edged with something fierce.

"Stop stalling, Win. Come on. Dance with me. You promised." His heated gaze telegraphed what kind of dance he thought this was going to be, and Winnie shuffled backwards slightly, out of his reach.

"I changed my mind."

The color rose in his cheeks. "You can't—"

"Sure she can, bud. Card declined, return to sender, application rejected. It's called consent, and you don't have it. Now run along and let us enjoy our evening, huh?"

Ethan surged forward, pressing himself into Winnie, turning her away from Daniel. "I'll tell her," he whispered. "I'll tell her what you did, Winnie."

"Back up," Daniel growled, shoving his shoulder between Winnie and Ethan, putting her behind him. Her ex was undeterred; he raised his voice.

"What do you think your mother would say if she knew the truth? If she knew the lengths you'd gone to in order to never become like her . . ."

"You wouldn't," she shot back.

"I don't want to, but you're leaving me no choice."

"And speaking of leaving, weren't you just?" Daniel quipped. Her ex kept her gaze hostage, unblinking as she considered his threat. But she'd had enough of this. Enough lies. Enough manipulation. Enough feeling small and out of control. She felt Daniel's hand slip into hers, warm and grounding, and it broke Ethan's spell. Winnie turned toward Daniel.

"You're a good man," she blurted out. "Thank you for showing me how a good man acts."

A slow smile slid across Daniel's face, and his eyes were twinkling.

Ethan's voice was low. "Winnie . . ."

"No," she said, keeping her eyes on her date. "Tell her if you want to. She's going to find out eventually anyway. I had hoped it would be a deathbed confession, but I did it, so I shouldn't hide it. I can live with it." She leaned to grab her clutch from the table, never releasing Daniel's hand. "I'm tired. Let's head up."

"Whatever you want," he said, tucking her hand into the crook of his arm to escort her from the ballroom. She didn't dare look back until they reached the elevators; Ethan wasn't following them.

Daniel squeezed her hand. "First of all, Deathbed Confession sounds like the name of an indie rock band from the nineties, and I may have to borrow it someday if my garage band ever has a revival tour." The elevator arrived, and they stepped inside. If he was trying to distract her, it was working. She was more than willing to go back to their everything-and-nothing conversations and give her heart a chance to stop trying to bash its way through her ribs.

"There's already a band called Dashboard Confessional, so I don't think it would market well. What did you play?"

"I sang, actually. Well, it was more of a yell if you ask my parents, but anyway . . ."

The doors slid open, and they wandered silently down the hall. He keyed their suite open, and his hand went immediately to his neck to loosen his tie. She started toward the bathroom when he caught her elbow.

"Winnie," he murmured, and it sent a tingle down her spine. She turned to face him. "You were amazing back there. I'm so incredibly proud of you." He pulled her into his arms, and she turned her head to rest it against his chest, listening to his heart pound. She pushed all the air out of her lungs, letting them deflate, letting go of the fear that had haunted her for months.

"That was hard."

"It seemed like it." They stood wrapped up together, warming each other against the chill of the room. "Can I ask you something?"

You can kiss me. I'd say yes. She leaned back to see him better, but his eyes showed that he was troubled, not in the mood for teasing. "What is it?"

"This thing he's got on you . . . how bad is it? You don't have to tell me, but I'll be honest: I'm concerned." He didn't need to say it; it showed in the way his mouth had tightened, his eyebrows snapping together.

She hesitated. If she was willing to kiss him, surely she should be willing to tell him this . . . but the last person she'd told was now downstairs planning to hold it against her. Still, Daniel wasn't Ethan. She wanted to trust him. And he'd trusted her with his dyslexia. That meant something to her. Everyone had secrets, but hers felt so much worse.

"You can't tell anyone . . ."

He made an X over his heart. "On my honor. Not a soul."

She let a deep breath out slowly, then let the truth go with the tail end of it. "I failed the MCATs on purpose. I never wanted to go to medical school."

He stared at her. "When you say you failed them on purpose, you mean . . ."

"Yes. I studied the correct answers and then picked the not-correct answers. Intentionally."

"Why?"

"Why?" she echoed, laughing a little. "Daniel, your family is so . . . so *nice*. Even Grumpy Kyle. They'd throw themselves off a bridge for you."

"Dr. Baker loves you, Fred."

"Yes, she does, but she also never accepted my father's death. And as such, I feel like she's just trying to start her life over through me, trying to get a different outcome this time.

It's not that I want to disappoint her, I just . . . can't be her. I don't want to be her."

"But why not just tell her the truth? Refuse to take the test?"

She shrugged one shoulder. "I thought this would be easier to swallow. Having a daughter who couldn't hack it was better than having a daughter who didn't love her enough to give it a try."

He pushed her hair back with both hands, letting his fingers sink into it at the back of her neck, and she melted into the feeling of being cared for. "It's not about love. You should get to choose your own adventure in life, choose what gives your life meaning. It's not unloving to want your own life."

"Just unloving to lie to her about it."

"You don't think she'll ever give up?"

She shook her head slowly, not wanting him to move away. "I would've thought after I failed the second time that she'd see that it was impossible. But not many people can tell my mother what's impossible."

"She does seem to know what she wants."

"In some areas. Not in others. All her dates have been disasters." Winnie stretched, and a yawn escaped her. Despite Daniel's lovely closeness, her brain and body were tapping out, but her heart was still frenetic with feelings . . .

"Will you . . ." She hesitated.

His voice pitched lower. "Will I what? Ask me, Winnie. Ask me for anything."

"Will you hold me?"

Without a word, he nodded, took off his jacket and tossed it onto the couch, then unbuttoned his sleeves and rolled them to his elbows. Winnie took his hand and led the way into her room, and his steps lagged slightly when he realized where she was going.

"This okay?"

"Yes." She kicked off her shoes and tossed back the comforter. Winnie lay down on the white sheets on her side so she could see the city out the window. He slotted in behind her, his fingers drifting up and down her arm. He smelled the same way he had the other day when she'd taken him home, and the familiarity of it was just the comfort she was looking for. Daniel pressed his face into her hair and sighed; she smiled.

Winnie turned to face him, and Daniel pulled her tighter into him, combing his fingers through her loose hair. They stared at each other; she suddenly felt wide awake, too busy cataloguing all the shades of blue in his eyes for sleep, too interested in watching the city lights move across the planes of his face to drop off to Dreamland.

"Do you have any medical conditions I don't know about?" he asked, his voice rough.

"Conditions?" she repeated, her own voice sounding vacant.

"Yes," he said. "Epilepsy, POTS, anything that would require you needing help in the night?"

She cocked a blonde eyebrow, then shook her head slowly.

"Good," he said, still stroking her hair soothingly. "Then will you do me a favor?"

"Anything," she said.

"Lock the door."

"Are you worried about drunken wedding guests stumbling in?"

He shook his head. "Not the front door. Your bedroom door. Lock it. And if you're wearing pajamas made of anything but cotton that covers you from your neck to your ankles, please use the hotel robes."

She couldn't help but grin. "Why, Dr. Durand, are you thinking about my anatomy?"

"Definitely." He smirked back. "But thinking's all I'm doing tonight." He leaned forward and gave her an innocent kiss on the cheek, and she'd never been more tempted to turn her head just a little and make it less innocent. He slid off the bed and headed for the door.

"Good night, Other Dr. Durand."

He paused in the doorway. "Good night, Winnie Baker. Sweet dreams."

CHAPTER
SEVENTEEN

THE NEXT MORNING, WINNIE poured herself some orange juice from a glass carafe. She stifled a yawn, lifting her glass to mask it, then took a sip. Ethan's unexpected threats, Daniel's murmured endorsements and her own rash declarations had had her tossing and turning well past one in the morning. It didn't look better in the light of an overcast Portland Sunday morning. She'd snuck out of the suite for brunch, letting Daniel stay passed out on the sofa; he hadn't bothered to pull out the bed, but he'd had a sheet over his chest . . . his bare chest. He had nice pecs, not too defined or too hairy, just very . . . nice. She'd stared at them for probably too long on her way to the bathroom this morning. But the time to herself had given her a chance to think. Why couldn't they be together? He was such a *nice* guy—thoughtful, funny, smart, tenacious. And even if he was a little younger, who was really going to notice? Maybe she was blowing it all out of proportion. They did work together, but it's not like she reported to him or vice versa. Maybe this could work.

"Winifred!" Her mentor's voice startled her out of her ponderings, and she hoped it didn't show. "You made it!" Dr. Weaver sat down next to her.

"Oh, Dr. Weaver, congrats! It was such a beautiful wedding. I apologize for not getting to spend the whole evening at the reception yesterday; I had a bit of trouble with . . ."

"Yes, I noticed. I thought you two were broken up?"

"We are. Only one of us got the memo."

"I see. No second-chance romance for you two, huh?"

"Definitely not. I regret the first chance." She didn't want to bring the conversation down. "But I'm so happy for you and Tim. And I'm so happy I could be here to celebrate with you."

Kari put an arm around her and gave her a friendly squeeze. "And I'm happy to see you moving on . . . robbing the cradle and everything. You cougar, you. Where is your handsome date, anyway? What's his name? Jail Bait?"

Winnie's stomach lurched at the implication; she'd never take advantage of someone like that, and it was disturbing even as a joke. "I wanted to let him sleep in. He doesn't get much opportunity. And his name is Daniel Durand." That made her wonder what his middle name was. Maybe she could ask him on the drive home, when they were alone again, just the two of them. "He's older than he looks, really." She chuckled, her face burning.

"He looks like he knows how to have fun, that's what he looks like."

To her surprise, Winnie's mind hit "Play" on the memory of driving him home that first time, him stealing her nachos. The Thor bobblehead. Even giving Jackson his shots.

"He does," she agreed, then stiffened as she realized what Dr. Weaver had meant, but Kari just laughed.

"Who cares if it's just a fling? Just enjoy yourselves. It's not like you're getting married."

"Right . . ." Winnie shifted her weight in her chair, trying to find a comfortable position for her legs, but unable to.

Dr. Weaver's eyebrows drew together, and she lowered her voice. "It *is* just a fling, right?"

"Of course. What else could it be? I needed a date, and he was available." She laughed uncomfortably, sipping her drink. Winnie's mouth tasted metallic, and she suddenly wanted something other than orange juice. She reached for a basket of cranberry-walnut scones. "Is everyone teasing you about babies?"

Dr. Weaver laughed out loud. "It's a bit late for that, isn't it? I'm in perimenopause already."

"Lucky."

"Just wait. You won't think so." Something over Winnie's shoulder caught Dr. Weaver's eye, and she grinned. "Here comes Sleeping Beauty."

"Sorry I'm late," Daniel greeted them, giving her shoulders an affectionate squeeze and the top of her head a quick kiss. Her heart beat a little faster. *Just an act. Just for today,* she reminded herself. "What'd I miss?"

"Nothing much," Dr. Weaver said, getting up. "Here, please, come sit by Winnie. I should go mingle anyway. Nice to meet you, Daniel."

Winnie passed him the mango, honeydew melon, and blueberry salad. Based on her limited observations of the man's eating habits, he needed as many vitamins and as much fiber as she could provide. She watched him fill his plate, and he gave her several sidelong glances, amusement turning up the corners of his mouth under his beard.

"Everything okay?"

"Yes."

"How'd you sleep?"

"Badly."

"Oh, I'm sorry. Why'd you sleep bad?"

She shrugged one shoulder. "Thinking."

"Speaking of which, any sign of your nemesis this morning?"

"No."

"Are you going to answer all my questions with just one word today?"

She smirked. "Maybe."

"What time did you want to leave this morning?"

Winnie shrugged. "Whenever."

Daniel chuckled as he sipped a cup of coffee one of the servers had poured for him. "When Winnie Baker commits to a scheme, look out, world."

She observed him as he ate; it was like watching a gazelle run for its life on *Planet Earth*. He wasn't messy, but he packed food away like a bear about to hibernate. What did he do with it all? Moreover, she wasn't the only one watching. A brunette in her early twenties one table over was whispering to her friend, casting glances in his direction, batting her eyelashes. Daniel was telling Winnie a story about getting a snowmobile stuck three years ago, and he didn't seem to notice the woman's overt attempts to get his attention.

"I'm sorry," she interrupted, "but do you know that woman? She's been staring at you."

Daniel turned to look, and the woman waved shyly. Daniel smiled and waved back with his fork. "No, I don't know her."

"Why's she waving, then?"

"Just friendly, I guess?" He took another bite of home-style potatoes. "I think I've got one of those familiar faces. Anyway, like I was saying . . ."

Flirting. That woman was flirting with her date right in front of her, because no one over thirty could possibly be dating Daniel. Dr. Weaver wasn't wrong: he did look young, younger than he really was, and the conservative way she dressed sometimes made Winnie seem older. The brunette flirter probably thought they were siblings or cousins or something—they did look somewhat similar. Winnie's heart was slowly sinking like a leaf in a swimming pool, just drifting down, down, down as the woman continued to make eyes at her oblivious friend. This was never going to work. Look at what Dr. Weaver had thought of them. Look at what this woman was assuming. No, her purpose here had been accomplished. They'd just be friends from here on out.

She stood up. "I need to finish up my packing. Are you all ready?"

He tapped his temple. "I played it smart. Never unpacked, so leaving is easy."

Winnie gave him a sad smile as she headed for the lobby's elevators. *No, leaving isn't easy. I wish I didn't know how warm the glow of your attention felt, even temporarily. I wish I'd never let you be my date, Daniel Durand. It was far too sweet to give up painlessly.*

CHAPTER
EIGHTEEN

WINNIE WAS QUIET ON the drive back to Timber Falls, staring out the passenger window. Daniel tried to engage her over medicine, babies, comic books, TV shows, anything, but he was still getting those same one-word answers. Something had happened at brunch, but he didn't know what, and he hadn't known how to bring it up earlier. By the time they got to Salem, he was officially distracted over it; he almost missed the exit to Detroit Lake, but thankfully, Winnie nudged him just in time. Daniel tried to curb his obsessive thoughts by watching the scenery as the packed suburbs and cookie-cutter cul-de-sacs faded into manufactured homes and long gravel driveways. Ford and Subaru replaced Audi and Lexus. Horses, sheep, and alpacas replaced fast-food restaurants and convenience stores.

Daniel glanced at her again; she was asleep. That was probably it. She was just tired. They'd had such a strong connection last night; he'd wanted to slap her stupid ex across the state. That kind of riling didn't happen to him very often, but one look into her fawn-brown eyes and his heart had calmed again. He never wanted anyone to mistreat her, try to manipulate her. Even as a friend, he wanted to have her back; he was glad she hadn't gone to the wedding alone out of pride or stubbornness.

Saying no seemed to be hard for her . . . unless she was saying no to him. He chuckled a little, mostly at himself. He'd never worked this hard for a date before. But he'd never felt about anyone the way he felt about Fred.

"Winnie? We're here," he said, shaking her shoulder gently.

She inhaled sharply as she came awake, looking around like she didn't know where she was, but her shoulders relaxed when she recognized his face, and it made him smile.

"You okay?"

She nodded, stretching, but didn't get out of the car. They sat in comfortable silence for a few moments.

"I had a good time."

"I had a good time, too," she said, massaging the fingers of one hand with the other.

"I'd like to see you again."

"You'll see me at the hospital," she said softly.

"Gosh, I was hoping for fewer sick people and more slow dancing . . ."

She gave him half a smile, but said nothing.

"What are you thinking, Win? I can't read you."

"I'll think about it."

Right. Well, it wasn't a no. He could work with a maybe, even if it wasn't the yes he was sure he'd get last night.

"Okay. I'll help you with your bag." He popped the trunk and got out just as Starla and her kids were coming down the apartment steps. She and Ainsley were close; it was partly their mutual love for books and part having grown up together. He'd always liked her, too; she set aside graphic novels for him at the library, for when he had time to read.

"Hey," he called. "You just gonna walk right by without saying hello?"

"Say hello to Dr. Durand," Starla instructed Aiden and Emily, and they obeyed. She opened the doors of the minivan remotely. "Go get in the car, please."

"Everything okay?" he asked, his voice low.

"Mostly. Just needed a little space from him today."

"Charlie's at your place?"

She shrugged one shoulder. "Don't know. Never came home last night. I didn't trust myself not to blow up when he finally waltzed in." Someone who didn't know the couple's tangled, thorny history might have expressed concern for Charlie's whereabouts, but Daniel knew better. That guy could take care of himself.

"You'll call me if you need anything?"

"Why?" Starla asked dryly. "You think you can tame my husband?"

"I think lions would be easier," he said, "but get me a whip and a chair, and I'll give it a shot." She laughed a little, and he squeezed her shoulders in a side hug. "Hang in there, Star."

"Don't have much of a choice," she said, backing toward her car with a wry grin. "Hey, Winnie."

"Hey, Starla. Thanks again for telling me about this place. I owe you big time."

"Hmm," Starla mused with a grin, "I'll have to remember that next time I give birth." Daniel's stomach turned; he hoped she wasn't really still sleeping with Charlie after all the crap he'd pulled. Every time the man cheated on her, he swore it was the last. Daniel had privately encouraged her to consider getting tested for STDs regularly. If that bastard gave her a lifelong illness, Daniel would break all the windows of his stupid Tahoe. And he'd only pay for half of the replacement afterward.

He carried Winnie's suitcase upstairs for her; Ainsley was just taking down the fort they'd built in the living room. She looked at her watch.

"Oh, you're home earlier than I thought. How'd it go?"

"Fine," Winnie said brightly, but Daniel seesawed his hand behind her back to say "sort of." "Thanks again, Daniel. I'll see you later."

"Okay," he muttered at her quickly retreating form as she disappeared down the hall toward the bedrooms.

"What happened?" Ainsley whispered, folding the plaid fleece blanket she was holding.

"Nothing. Everything was going great last night, but then this morning..."

Ainsley's gaze narrowed. "What kind of great?"

"Give me a little credit. It was our first date."

"Didn't seem to matter to you much in the past," she muttered, and he gave her a sheepish grin.

"I did not sleep with her, Slick. I didn't even try. I swear."

"Okay, I'm just saying. She's my friend and she's a great roommate. Do not scare her off."

"I did not—fine. Whatever. I'm leaving." He wasn't really mad, and Ainsley would know that. He was, however, ready to be alone with his own thoughts, which was why he changed into his biking gear as soon as he got home. He was just about to close the garage door when his phone rang.

"Hey," his dad said, and Daniel could hear the rest of his family in the background. He'd already bowed out of family dinner; hopefully, they hadn't forgotten. He heard a door close behind him, and the noise disappeared.

"Hey. What's up?"

"Just wanted to see how it went with the midwife."

"Winnie. And it went . . . okay." He sighed. "Can I call you later? I was just about to go for a ride."

"Oh, great. I'll join you. See you in ten."

"Wait, Dad, I actually just wanted—" It was too late. His dad had already hung up. With a growl, Daniel stabbed a finger into the keypad to close the door and mounted the bike, making his way through town to his parents' house.

His dad was waiting for him out front, smiling like nothing was wrong. Daniel didn't even stop, just circled in front of the house while Evan got on his bike and trusted that he'd follow. He got on the old railroad path that ran along the river and started up the hill toward the falls. They didn't talk for the first four miles. As his heart rate went up, his resentment went down. It felt good to breathe deep; it wasn't even raining. It wasn't sunny, but that felt like too much to ask, and besides, the gray matched his mood. His dad didn't break the silence until they stopped at the bathrooms at Timber Falls State Park; Daniel hadn't thought to bring any water, which showed how badly this was messing with his head.

"She didn't agree to a second date?"

"Nope. Said she'd think about it, though."

"That's rough. I'm sorry."

Daniel grunted.

"You going all the way to the falls?"

"I was planning to, but if you need to turn back . . ."

"Nope. Mom's roasting chickens. No grill necessary."

"You're still ignoring your other family members."

His dad stepped closer, taking off his helmet to run a microfiber towel over his short hair. "I'm hanging out with my son when he needs me. They understand."

Daniel wanted to retort that he was neither needed nor invited, but he didn't want to hurt his feelings. And it wasn't true, anyway; all his thoughts came spilling out as they exited the parking lot.

"I don't get why she's making this so difficult. She's not that much older than I am, but she acts like it's this huge barrier to us being together."

His dad nodded slowly. "It's a double standard, isn't it? If you date a younger person, you're applauded. If she does it, she's called a cougar or worse. As if falling in love with someone who arrived on earth a few years after you is somehow predatory."

"I mean, it could be, obviously, but we're both adults."

"Right. I can understand why you're frustrated. But you're not the one who's taking a risk. She is."

"So how do I make it easier for her? She likes me, Dad. I saw it in her eyes. She wants to be with me."

His dad shrugged and the bike weaved momentarily. "Keep giving her attention. Keep thinking about her and the things she likes. Keep giving yourself. She may change her mind."

Neither of them were in shape enough to talk through the climb up the steep asphalt path to the top of the waterfalls, but they stopped when they got there. Daniel liked to watch the water hurl itself over the edge, the leaves and sticks swept along with it, droplets flinging up into a fine spray even now, when the water level was low.

"I'm not giving up," he panted, "not until she says no."

His dad leaned over to punch him lightly on the shoulder. "I'm rooting for you," Evan replied, and they watched the waterfall for a minute before silently turning to begin the trip back down. When they pulled up to his parents' house, his dad turned to him. "Will you come in for dinner? I'm sure Mom made plenty."

Daniel shook his head. "I'm all sweaty and stuff. I'll see them next week."

Evan's smile said he understood, and Daniel waved as he continued on to his house. He noticed the manila envelope under the welcome mat before he was close enough to see what it was. Throwing down his bike in the grass, he leaped up the front step and snatched it out. Her handwriting was not easy to read, but he was determined.

This seemed a fitting thank you gift, especially after you stayed so calm in the face of Ethan's nonsense. I really did have fun. Thanks again.

–Fred

Pulling out the comic book, he grinned. *Incredible Hulk* #319, Bruce Banner marries Betty Ross. He already owned it, of course, but this copy was going on his nightstand where he could see it first thing when he woke up in the morning. It was a reminder to keep calm and carry on. A reminder that it wasn't over yet.

CHAPTER
NINETEEN

NOT A LOT OF MIDWIVES and a whole lot of patients meant that Winnie was slammed with work the next week. Three nights in a row, she was up with a laboring mother. She was fairly sure her blood was more coffee than plasma at this point. Frances Mitton, the other midwife who worked at Santiam, had gone to Dallas to take care of her sister, who'd just had knee surgery.

Monday was her birthday. She found an e-card from her mother in her email inbox, spent an hour and a half convincing a nervous patient that she was just having Braxton Hicks contractions, and assisted a doctor-led birth that led to her getting vomited on when the patient had a reaction to the drugs they'd given her. Given her fatigue and just not having time to sort out her muddled feelings, Winnie actively avoided Daniel, ducking into supply closets and break rooms when she saw him coming. She felt bad about it, but she just didn't have time. He'd forget about her eventually and move on to someone else . . . although the gifts said otherwise. On Wednesday, she found a bar of Green & Black's sea salt chocolate in her mailbox. On Thursday, there was lavender hand lotion; she'd used it on a patient a few hours later with good results. On Friday, there was a pair of pink yoga toe socks with anti-skid dots on the bottoms and a typed note: "Thinking of you. Hope you've had a great week." Martina saw her clutching them.

"More gifts? He's persistent."

Winnie swallowed hard and nodded, grinning despite herself.

Martina slammed her locker shut. "What's holding you back? You like him. I know you do."

"He's too young for me."

Her friend stared at her blankly. "What are you talking about?"

"I just mean, he's still in his twenties, and I'm..."

"Winifred." Martina's look could not be more cross. "Stop acting like you're ancient. You're not. There's not one thing wrong with dating him. Seriously."

Something eased in Winnie's chest, despite her friend's irritation. She was right; it was her insecurity talking. She knew it, but it helped to hear it so plainly from someone else's lips.

"And he's oblivious," Winnie added, trying to deflect from her embarrassment.

She snorted. "Most people are. Look at me, I dated my high school sweetheart for years, thinking we were moving toward marriage, and then . . ." She held her hand out, empty. "Our first real conversation in years, and I realized that we wanted different things." She pulled out a lip gloss and applied it in the mirror. "At least he's being up front with you. At least he knows what he wants."

ON SATURDAY, AFTER a long, difficult birth, her mother caught her in the hallway. "I would like you to come over and help me pick out new flooring for the beach house. Since it's going to be yours someday, I thought you might like to have some input, and you have an eye for such things. Would you have time tonight?"

"Oh, Mom, I'm really exhausted, I don't know that I'd . . ." The hurt look in her mother's eyes made her swallow her objections like a horse tablet. "Sure. I can stop by for a few minutes."

A few minutes turned into an hour, and Winnie was fighting to keep her eyes open as her mother scrolled through the bamboo flooring in various shades and finishes.

"I also really need to nail down some sessions to help you study for the MCATs, Winifred; I don't understand why you haven't arranged it yet."

Winnie hesitated. It was better if her mom heard it from her than from Ethan, and she had no reason to think that he wouldn't make good on his threats from the previous weekend. Was that only a week ago? It felt like a lifetime.

Winnie took a deep breath. "I'm not taking the MCATs."

Sandra turned to her sharply. "You missed the deadline to sign up? Oh, for God's sake, Winifred, I reminded you over and over. How could you be so careless?"

"I didn't miss the deadline. I'm just not taking them."

Sandra stilled. The room was silent. Her mother stared at her.

"Well, that's just silly. You can't get into medical school if you don't—"

"I'm not going to medical school." Though her voice was steady, her whole body trembled with the absolute enormity of what she'd just pronounced, the utter havoc it was about to release on her relationship with her mom, like she'd just opened the front door to a herd of stampeding elk. She couldn't stop shaking, and no amount of deep breathing seemed to help. "I'm not going to medical school. I'm happy being a midwife. I never wanted to be a doctor; that's what you wanted."

Her mother looked around, as if searching for someone to confirm this was really happening. *In for a penny, in for a pound . . .*

"And I failed the tests on purpose."

For a split second, Winnie thought her mother might not do it. Might not go cold, might not let her fury at being lied to eclipse the fact that her daughter needed her. Might let her guard down just enough to try to understand Winnie's perspective, might step back for a moment to *see her*. The broken, introspective look that crossed her mother's face for the briefest second allowed hope to swell in Winnie's heart. Then Sandra lifted her gaze.

"I think you should go."

That hope dissipated in an instant. Winnie felt her heart desiccating inside her, shriveling up like a popped balloon.

"All right." Quietly, she gathered her purse and coat and slipped on her shoes. "I'll see you on Sunday." Her mother was still staring at the piano when she closed the door behind herself.

Winnie got in her car, numb. She wanted to go back inside and run upstairs to her old room, but apparently, she wasn't welcome here at the moment. Her grandparents . . . no. That wasn't right. The apartment would be dark and cold. But maybe . . . maybe Daniel would be home. She wanted him to hold her again, like he'd done at the hotel. He could help diffuse this tightness in her chest, this panic.

She let her body tip forward until her forehead rested on the steering wheel. She'd been avoiding him since their awkward drive home on Sunday. It wasn't ideal. She hadn't planned this well. She hadn't planned to need Daniel Durand at all, but he'd made himself indispensable when she wasn't paying attention. God, he was sneaky.

It didn't take long to drive to his house, despite the rain. She trudged up the front steps of the shared house and knocked on the front door. No one answered. Maybe he wasn't home, maybe he was at work. She knocked again, harder.

Daniel opened the door, wearing heather-gray sweatpants that hung off his trim hips and a navy-blue T-shirt with a golf ball–sized hole near the bottom hem.

"Winnie." He looked around, as though she might have someone else with her. "What are you doing here?"

"Can I come in?" She pushed her way past him into the house and down the hall toward the living room. A young woman's voice with a light Canadian accent filled the space as she carefully enunciated a list of symptoms of a fourteen-year-old girl, including anxiety and bilateral leg weakness. Daniel picked up the remote and turned off the stereo his phone was plugged into. "What are you listening to?"

"Peds Cases podcast. It's a good way to . . . absorb information. For me." He ran a hand through his hair; it wasn't pulled back, and he was wearing square black-rimmed glasses. They weren't quite giving her a Clark Kent vibe, but not everything about him could be heroic.

"Is Kyle here?" Based on the medical textbooks spread out all over the hardwood floor, the half-empty chip bowl, open jar of salsa and empty bottles of that weird imported soda he liked, she knew the answer already.

"No, he's at my parents'. Helping my dad install a sound system or something nerdy. He'll be back soon."

"How soon?"

"Um, I'm not sure. Did you want to wait for him? Is there something I can help you with?" His voice was careful, and the way he shifted his weight and avoided her gaze told her he was uncomfortable. She hadn't exactly been forthcoming about where they stood. She would fix that now.

Nodding to herself, Winnie took her coat off. "Lie down."

Daniel stilled. "Pardon?"

"I said, lie down," she said, pulling her hair down, relishing the feeling of letting it tumble down her back, and kicking off her shoes. He stared at her as she carefully hung her purse on the back of the white kitchen chair.

"Sorry, what's happening right now?" he said, still not moving.

"You're going to lie down on the couch for me. Now." She gave him the reproachful glare she usually reserved for mothers who wouldn't give her the baby to be weighed because they

were too busy bonding. Getting their vitals was a necessity, unfortunately. So was lying down with Daniel, feeling his arms
around the ribs that caged her poor, cracked heart.

Not taking his eyes off her, he backed toward the couch
and lay down on it, with one hand behind his head. That was
a mistake on his part; it made his bicep look amazing. Like, so
amazing that she wanted to bite it like one of those turkey legs
at the fair. She must've made a noise that she wasn't aware of,
because he sat up, leaning on his elbows.

"Are you okay?" he asked slowly. "You're acting . . . weird."

"No," she said, clearing her throat. At least his beautiful bicep was at a safer angle now. "I am not okay. I am very not
okay."

"What happened?"

"I told Dr. Baker that I am not going to medical school."

"And she didn't take it well?"

She felt the end of her nose tingling, and she knew the tears
were coming. "No," she whispered. "She did not. So I need you
to lie down so you can hold me."

He went backwards so fast, it was like someone hit the re-
cline button on an airplane seat, and she snort-laughed as she
wiped a tear away. He opened his arms, staring up at her, his
eyes big and so genuinely sad for her. Winnie slotted herself into the space between his body and the back of the couch, and
he settled his arms around her shoulders, squeezing her briefly.
After a moment's hesitation, she relaxed against his chest, feeling it rise and fall under her cheek, listening to his steady heart-
beat. Winnie wiped another tear and released a shaky sigh.

"Oh, Fred," he murmured against her hair. "I'm so sorry."

"It's okay."

"No, it's not okay. She has no right. It's your life. Being a midwife is your calling." He began to rub her back. "It makes me want to go down there and give her a piece of my mind."

Winnie sat up quickly, her hand pressed to his chest. "Tell me you're not going to do that."

He grimaced. "I can't just say nothing."

"Yes, you can. I didn't come here for a white knight; I just needed some comfort."

He wrapped a bit of her hair around his index finger, rubbing it between his fingers. "And I'm comfortable?"

"Yes," she said simply. To her surprise, the warmth in his eyes died a little. "Isn't that a good thing?"

"I don't know," he muttered.

"You'd rather I be uncomfortable with you?"

"Well, no, but . . ." Daniel sighed. "I just . . . never mind. Now's not the time to talk about this."

Without thinking, she slid down so they were chest to chest and stroked his beard. "I'll be so sad when you have to do surgery."

"Because someone is sick?"

"Well, that. But also, we say goodbye to the beard. I love the beard."

"It always comes back," he said, leaning into her lazy touch, his eyes closing. Those full pink lips . . . it was just too tempting. He looked so perfect, even with his hair askew, his thick glasses instead of his contacts. And with his eyes closed, he jumped a little as their lips met. She pulled back, embarrassed. Of course he didn't want that. She'd been ignoring him for days, and now to think that she could just show up here and make out with him was ridiculous. And she should've asked first instead of surprising him.

She was still thinking that as she started to push herself up off him, already thinking about where her shoes were, when he sprang into action: his legs wrapped around hers to keep her there, his chest came up to meet hers, his hands came to her shoulders, pulling her down, and his lips . . . his lips were doing things that made her feel like her whole body was overheating. She felt like she couldn't get close enough to him, even though they were pressed together everywhere. He must've felt the same, because he wrapped his arms around her, holding her against him, still kissing the daylights out of her. Daniel made little grunts when she caught his tongue between her teeth, and she sighed softly when his hands drifted down her sides.

"If I have to get a bucket of water to separate you two, I'm going to be unhappy."

Winnie sat up so fast that she nearly toppled off the couch onto the floor and took Daniel with her, her head spinning. "Dr. Durand." Where had Kyle come from? How the heck had they not heard the garage door? "I'm so s-sorry," she stammered.

"For what?" he asked, frowning. "I was just kidding. And if you're dating my brother, you can call me Kyle."

"No, I . . . I need to go."

It appeared Daniel was still recovering from the shock as well, and consequently, he'd let his grip on her relax, so she seized the opportunity to extricate herself. She shoved her feet into her boots and threw her coat over her arm.

"Winnie, seriously," Kyle said, pacing after her. "I was just kidding. Stay. I obviously interrupted something . . . important. I'll just go upstairs."

"No, it's fine," she said, twisting her hair into a sloppy bun as she bolted toward the entryway. "I have to go anyway."

"Win. Wait." She already had the front door open when Daniel caught up with her. "Wait, wait, wait."

It was raining hard; she had to stop and put her coat on if she didn't want to get soaked. *Stupid rain. Stupid beard. Stupid heart.*

"Your heart is not stupid," Daniel said gruffly, turning her to face him. She hadn't meant to say that out loud . . . She stared up at him under the awning, sure of so little, but sure that she wanted to look at his dumb face, even when it was scowling at her.

"It doesn't know what it wants. That's pretty stupid."

He gently drew her back inside by her elbow. "It doesn't have to know right now, does it? Give it time. It can't be all stupid if it wanted to kiss the guy who's crazy about you." He led her over to the kitchen table, and she looked around warily; Kyle was nowhere to be seen.

"I guess not." She sat down and he pulled up a chair next to her.

"Let me cook you dinner. You've had a crap day. Just let me feed you, then you can go home."

"People usually make out at the end. We're doing everything backwards. It's like a reverse date."

He grinned. "Then let's lean into it." Going into the kitchen, she heard him rummaging around in the freezer, and a moment later, he returned with a half gallon of Tillamook's

Udderly Chocolate ice cream, a scooper, two bowls and two spoons. "Dessert first, then dinner."

She tilted her face up to see him better. "You're a bad influence, Dr. Durand."

He dropped a sweet kiss on her lips. "Live a little, Nurse Baker."

"I think I'll have to, if I'm going to spend time with you," she said, pulling her bowl toward her.

Daniel's phone whooshed with a text message, and he checked it, then laughed.

"What?"

"Kyle wants to know if it's safe to come downstairs." Daniel held his spoon in his mouth as he quickly typed back with two thumbs and pressed "Send."

"What'd you say?"

He bounced his eyebrows and removed the spoon. "I said only if he didn't mind watching us feed each other. He sent back a barf emoji. I don't think we have to worry about him coming down anytime soon."

Winnie snickered. "Don't be naughty, this is his house."

"Hey, I pay rent when I remember. There's nothing in my lease about not making out with a beautiful woman in the living room." His eyebrows danced again suggestively. "Or in the kitchen, for that matter . . ."

"Your own brother made you sign a lease?"

Daniel nodded as he took another spoonful. "It contains information about quiet hours, the equitable splitting of utilities, dish responsibilities, my contributions toward yard work, plus a clause about renter's insurance. I ignore most of it."

"Very thorough," she said. "Ainsley just showed me where I could put my bathroom stuff and left me to fend for myself. She doesn't even remember to get my half of the rent most of the time."

"That sounds about right."

Winnie paused as she angled her spoon for a chocolate chunk. "Did you and she ever . . ."

"Did we ever what?" Daniel asked, scooting his chair closer to hers. "Did we ever eat ice cream together?"

She felt a blush creeping up her neck. "Yeah."

"Nope. We tried kissing once when we were about thirteen. It was like kissing my sister or something. I don't think we were just bad at it . . . it just wasn't there." He swallowed. "In other words, it was nothing like kissing you."

"Flirt," she said, setting her spoon on the table. "Take that away, please, and get me some real food."

"As you wish," he winked, rising to put the carton away.

Oh dear. Especially with his hair flopping in his face like that, there was something a bit Westley-ish about him, and now she'd never be able to unsee that. Did he even know what he was quoting?

"Do you like that movie?" he called from the kitchen.

She smiled. "I've never been in a land war in Asia," she called back. "What do you think?"

They eventually coaxed Kyle into sharing their frozen lasagna, but he went upstairs again when she picked up a book to quiz Daniel on pediatric-specific illnesses. After he changed and put his contacts in, Daniel walked her home, all the way up the stairs to the apartment door. He leaned on the doorframe as she unlocked it.

"Can I come in?" he asked, his gaze heated, but Winnie shook her head.

"Reverse date, remember?" She smiled. "All you can do is kiss me like it's a hello."

He shuffled forward, taking her face in his hands. "Then I'm going to pretend I haven't seen you in days." Somehow, they were still kissing when she heard footsteps on the stairs behind them.

"Starla?" Winnie looked at her phone; it was nearly midnight.

In the dim porch light, Winnie couldn't see the tears on Starla's face until she was two feet away, but regardless, the slump of her shoulders, her rumpled clothing, and the dejected cadence of her footfalls had already given away that something was amiss.

"Anybody on your couch tonight?" she asked, running a hand through her dark hair, then twisting it to squeeze the water out.

"Did you walk here?"

She bobbed her head, then hugged her middle, and Winnie's heart cracked at how defeated she looked. Winnie glanced at Daniel, who looked like he was biting back words and perhaps saving punches for someone who wasn't there.

"Well, come in, let's get you dry and warm," Winnie said, ushering her into the apartment. There was no sign of Ainsley, so Winnie dug around in the linen closet until she found a towel and an extra quilt and blanket for the couch. "Can I make you a cup of tea?"

"Sure," Starla said. She pressed her face into the towel for a long moment.

"I've got some extra PJs you can borrow."

"Okay."

Daniel had followed them in, and he stood by the doorway with his arms crossed, scowling. "Star, do we need to call the sheriff? Where are your kids?"

"Cheating's not illegal," Starla said matter-of-factly, sitting down hard on the couch. "And the kids are asleep at home. I'll be back before they wake up. Don't worry, Charlie wouldn't leave them alone. He loves *them*." She covered her face with both hands, and Winnie watched as Daniel crossed to the couch and sat next to her to hold her around her shaking shoulders. She searched inside for a sense of jealousy, but couldn't find anything but respect. She liked how much he cared about other people. This was obviously some kind of ongoing thing for Starla, but he wasn't judging her. No one around here seemed to have anything bad to say about Starla. The same could not be said about Charlie.

The kettle whistled and Winnie moved quickly to turn it off. Ashwagandha tea would've been her first choice; it was good for agitation and stress and was what she'd give Starla if she were recovering from a difficult birth. But a failing marriage was not the same. She rummaged through their meagre selection: chamomile would be soothing without keeping her awake. She had no idea what to do for this situation except try to comfort her. She placed the mug in front of Starla, putting a light hand on her shoulder.

"Where's *my* tea?" Daniel demanded, his mock outrage making both women smile.

"You have not been invited to stay," Winnie reminded him. "You should go home and sleep."

"Fine, I see how it is," he said, standing up and putting his hands on his narrow hips. "But this apartment clearly has sexist and discriminatory policies on overnight guests. See if I make out with you again next time you're upset."

Starla pivoted to give Winnie a wide-eyed look, and Daniel stage-whispered to her, "I will, though. She's an amazing kisser, and I like her a lot. I'd kiss her no matter what." If Winnie hadn't already been blushing fiercely, that would've done it.

"Hey," Winnie started, "don't—"

"Fine," he said, holding up his hands in a show of innocence. "You don't want Starla to know your superpower, fine. But I'm onto you, lady," he said, pointing at her with a grin as he shut the front door behind him.

"Well, well, well." Ainsley stood in the hallway in a hoodie that said, "Someone in Timber Falls Loves Me" and plaid PJ pants, grinning widely. "Isn't this a fun development?"

"Did we wake you? I'm sorry, I should've heated the water in the microwave," Winnie said, fussing with the blankets to attempt to distract the two women staring at her from what had just happened.

"No, I just got up to pee and saw the lights on. Welcome back, Starla. Winnie, you've been making out with Daniel Durand?"

"Just the once . . . ," she said, crossing back to the kitchen to wipe something down. Anything, really. There had to be stray drops of water or crumbs somewhere.

"Well, you might as well put that kettle back on," said Ainsley, sitting down on the couch. "Because we need *the tea*, sister." After her discussion on age with Daniel, Winnie had done a hasty search of common millennial phrases, and this was one that had to do with needing information—especially somewhat scandalous information.

"Yeah," Starla said, a shy smile breaking the mask of fatigue and pain she'd been wearing up until now. "I want details, too." That did it. If it would make Starla happy on what was obviously a terrible night, she'd sacrifice her pride and share.

"Well, first of all," she said, "do you know what a reverse date is?"

CHAPTER TWENTY

"DON'T PEEK," HE SAID, covering her eyes with one hand. He'd been quick to invite her over again after their reverse date, and he was excited for her to see his belated birthday surprise.

"How could I peek? You're covering my whole face with your giant hand." She sniffed. "Which smells like fish, by the way. What have you been doing, whippersnapper, and do I want you touching me?"

He let his warm breath drift onto her neck near her ear. "I'm pretty sure you always want me touching you . . ." She shivered a little, turning her head into his neck, and it was very gratifying to know he was reading her right.

"Not if it's going to make me reek like week-old salmon," she replied primly, and he chuckled as he guided her down the hall.

"Don't you trust me, Fred? Would I do that to my friend on her belated birthday celebration?"

She wrinkled her nose at the moniker.

"You said I couldn't call you my girl, and calling you my woman sounded so patronizing. So this is on you. Come up with something better and I'll use it." Their slow shuffle down the hall finally halted near the kitchen. "Okay, you can look now."

She blinked as her eyes adjusted to being open again. Candlelight bathed the kitchen table, on which were two cream plates with gold edges, a small vase of daisies between them, two V-shaped metal tools, and a couple of tiny two-tined forks. A large empty glass mixing bowl sat on the side closest to them for the shells, and each place setting had a small bowl of a sunny yellow liquid that looked like melted butter. But the real attraction was what sat on each plate.

"You bought . . . crab?" Her expression was blank.

Uh-oh.

He rubbed her upper arms, as if he could coax a reaction out of her. "Yeah, you mentioned how much you loved it a few weeks ago, how you'd always had it with your dad when you were a kid. I know things are kind of weird in your family right now, so I thought I'd try to recreate a special memory for you."

Winnie's face went soft. "Oh. Thank you." She swallowed. "There's just one problem."

"What's that?"

"I have no idea how to eat a whole crab. My dad always cracked mine for me."

"Oh." Daniel rubbed his clean-shaven chin thoughtfully. "Well. Hmm. Well, hey, how hard could it be? We can figure this out, right? That's what YouTube is for."

"Ah, yes. YouTube. The millennial's duct tape."

He chuckled softly, then led her over to the table. "Don't knock YouTube, Fred. That's how I learned to fix my bike, turn off the water at my parents' beach house at the street, change the oil in my car, bake zucchini bread. YouTube is my every-thing."

"I see. Well, pull it up, then. Let's see if it can save this dinner."

Daniel pulled his phone out of his back pocket and sat down as he opened the app. Winnie leaned over his shoulder to see better. That was nice, but he wanted her closer. He could see down her shirt a little, but he forced his attention to stay on the screen.

"Let's see . . . Coastal Loving should know, right? That sounds credible."

"That's Coastal *Living*, Dr. Durand. Coastal Loving would be something else entirely."

He laughed, but Winnie suddenly looked chagrined. She must have realized that she'd hit on one of his weaknesses by correcting his reading. It hadn't bothered him in the slightest, but he could see that she was troubled.

He pulled her around the chair. "You can't see back there. Come up here and learn so I don't have to do this for you. As you so kindly pointed out, I already smell fishy." He patted his leg, and Winnie's mouth dropped open.

"What was that?" She imitated his motion on his leg, and he grinned.

"Come sit with me so you can see." He patted it again, his eyebrows bouncing.

"I haven't sat on anyone's lap since I was six, and even then, I didn't get the pink scooter I asked for. Jolly old elf, my eye." *Don't laugh, don't laugh.* He pinned her with a sultry stare, and she shuffled farther away from him. "I'm too heavy."

He shifted his hips forward, making his lap bigger, waiting.

"You are ridiculous," she muttered, crossing her arms.

"That's interesting," he said, rubbing his leg slowly, like he was warming it up for her. "Wanting to be close to you doesn't *feel* ridiculous . . ."

She hugged herself tighter. "Adults don't sit like that."

"A. That's not true. And B. Who's going to know?"

Winnie sighed and let her arms drop limply to her sides as she meandered closer to him. "This is only because I'm hungry," she said, carefully lowering herself to balance on his right leg. "This isn't because I'm on board with your childish—"

He pulled her close and kissed her, craving her taste again; he'd been replaying their hot make-out session nonstop in his mind. Her lips were soft against his, and when she opened her eyes, she looked a bit dazed in the best way. "You have a lot of things you don't do," Daniel murmured.

"That's true," she murmured back, kissing him again.

"Why is that?"

"Why?" she repeated, and the storm in her eyes told him she was trying to find the right words. "I think . . ." She faltered. Winnie looked into his eyes; he was trying to stay present in her discomfort, watching her, just listening, his arms wrapped around her hips, his fingers drawing light circles on her leg. *Give her yourself,* Dad had said. He was sure as hell trying.

She swallowed. "I think it's because of my dad. Sometimes, when someone who was important to you dies, their family and friends have this epiphany about how life is short and they get a burning desire to carpe diem. They write that novel, or build that treehouse or start that shelter for homeless cats or whatever that they've always dreamed of." She rubbed the short, soft hair at the back of his neck. "I think I sort of had the opposite reaction. I didn't want to carpe anything. I wanted to retreat from life, to be safe; I think that's why graphic novels appealed to me. They still contained the drama of life, but they made the world right when I felt . . . left hanging. My mother withdrew from me, and deep down, I felt that I was on my own from now on."

Daniel nodded slowly, his gaze never leaving her face. "So you became a midwife. And for all those babies, you're helping make sure that they're safe and cared for and attached, making sure their mamas are there to bond with them. You're rewriting your story, one birth at a time."

Winnie stared at him, and her mouth dropped open. "I honestly never thought of it that way."

Daniel kissed her. "That's because you're the heroine. The heroine never thinks about herself. That's the sidekick's job."

"Is that what you are? My sidekick?"

"I'd like to apply, yes."

"The vetting process is lengthy, just so you know."

"Oh?" He shifted under her, pulling her closer.

"Yes, it's multidimensional, very involved."

"Is there any reading involved?" Her crestfallen expression told him she wasn't ready to joke about his dyslexia yet. He should've known better.

"No," she whispered. "Unless you count reading me like a book."

"That kind of reading comes easy. Unlike the letters on the page, you don't jump around like fleas when I look at you."

"What do you see when you look at me?"

"A mind that can do six things at once. A compassionate heart that can always make people comfortable. A spirit that exudes joy. Not to mention eyes like lava cake, a smile that knocks me off my feet . . ."

"You don't think I'm a coward?"

"No," he said gently. "I think you're fighting one battle at a time. And there's nothing wrong with that. Even Wonder Woman tries to take on one villain at a time." He paused, watching her carefully. "You've been pulling out that lasso of truth more often lately, huh?"

She nodded ruefully. "It was overdue."

"How does it feel?"

"It feels amazing. And it hurts. And I'm relieved. And I'm disgusted that it took so long, and I'm thankful that I summoned the courage. And I'm lost to undo the damage I've done."

He tipped his head to look behind her, then leaned to look in front of her. "Where are you keeping this cornucopia of feelings, Wonder Woman?"

"I honestly do not know," she laughed. Winnie's stomach gurgled, and she pressed a hand to her belly as if to rebuke it. The butter was starting to congeal, too, even though he'd turned up the thermostat from the glacial temperatures Kyle kept it at.

"I think we'd better watch this video."

"Yeah, I think so." She pushed her face closer to his to see the screen better; he could've cast it to the TV, but he wasn't going to reveal that. It was so cute how she never thought of things like that, and this was far better, anyway. She smelled like lavender again . . . She felt so good, pressed against him. He propped up the phone against the flower vase to have his hands free. This was Dungeness crab, not snow crab like the first one demonstrated, but that guy had a cute little wooden mallet with a bottle opener on the end.

"Why don't we have mallets?" Winnie asked.

"Because Ainsley didn't give me any."

"Maybe we should call . . ."

"No, no, no! If I call her, she's going to come over and try to show us how to do this." Her eyebrows high, her mouth puckered, Winnie watched him with eyes wide as he ranted. He didn't care. "Then she'll want a glass of wine, and then this won't be a date! This is a date, dammit. We can *do this*, Winnie Baker, we *will* do this—we will prevail over these crustaceans!"

"Are you done?"

"Yes."

She picked up his crab and cracked it in half with her bare hands, squirting them with juice. They both yelled, then she leaned over, laughing into his neck, and it was the best feeling he'd had all week. She picked up the pick, carefully worked a large hunk of meat out, and dipped it into the butter.

"Well, look at you, cracking crab like a real Oregonian . . ." The joke died on his lips as she brought the bite to them, holding one hand under it to catch the butter as it languidly dripped from the crab. Desire fluttered in his belly; automatically, his mouth fell open, and Daniel pulled the crab from the fork with his teeth. He watched as she did the same for herself and let her think that it was the taste of the cold, tender meat paired with the warm, salty butter that had him groaning. Winnie grimaced, holding her hands out in front of her, palms down, fingers spread wide, as if she had nail polish drying. "I think I need a napkin."

Without overthinking it, Daniel caught her wrist and brought her buttery fingers to his lips, watching her eyes for confirmation that this was wanted . . . and based on the look she was giving him, she was listening to a debate tournament between propriety and passion in her head. "Can I help you out?" he asked, keeping his voice low. He could feel the trembling in her fingers as she nodded. He needed to go slow, he reminded himself. In the past, he'd always rushed into the physical part of a relationship like a linebacker. With Winnie, it felt more like tiptoeing; she'd been burned by the last guy, and he didn't want to scare her off.

Holding her gaze, he brought her first finger to his lips and sucked off the butter slowly, swirling his tongue around the tip of it. He watched as her cheeks heated and her lips parted, and Daniel suddenly knew what he wanted for every Christmas for the rest of his life: getting to watch Winnie's face while he turned her on.

Down the hall, a door slammed. "Why does it smell like fish in here?"

Winnie jumped up, pulling back her hand like she'd been burned. She managed to land her backside in her own seat and pick up the crab crackers before Kyle came into the room.

"Oh. That's why." His brother ran a hand through his dark hair, looking around. "Sorry, I'll, um . . ."

"I thought you were going to Philip's tonight . . ." He kept his eyes on his plate so he didn't accidentally murder Kyle with his gaze. He felt like it was entirely possible that he could shoot laser beams out of his corneas right now. This was the second time he'd ruined a moment when he and Winnie were getting closer.

"Yeah, that didn't work out. Cooper's sick, so they stayed home."

"It's fine," Winnie said, sipping her wine. "How was your day, Kyle?"

"Frustrating." He opened the hall closet and shoved his backpack inside. "I spent most of the day trying to diagnose a patient's chest pain, and it turned out he was just dehydrated."

"I empathize," she said, rising as she grabbed both their butter bowls. "One of my patients is having high blood pressure, and she's resisting the medication to bring it down."

"What are her other symptoms?" Kyle asked, leaning his hip against the doorway to the kitchen. "You know, I just read that women with stage 1 high blood pressure during their first trimester had 2.5 times greater risk associated with developing preeclampsia."

Winnie frowned. "Yes, I read that, too. I'm concerned about her, but I'm not sure what more I can do."

Frowning. She was frowning now, thinking about work, just when he'd finally gotten her to think about something else. This would not fly.

"That's a bummer," Daniel said. "Kyle, can I talk to you for a minute upstairs?"

"Sure. Can I just—"

Daniel put his hands on his hips. "No. I'll be right back, Fred."

Her amused glance told him that she had an inkling about what their conversation might entail. "You want your butter heated?"

"That'd be great, thanks." Daniel thundered up the narrow carpeted stairway; Kyle came up slower, his expression wary.

"Twice. Twice now, you've interrupted us."

Kyle nodded. "I'd just like to point out that you do have a bedroom in the house . . ."

"I don't want to eat crab in my bedroom!"

"Fair enough, but for other activities . . ."

"She's not ready for bedroom activities. But she's very ready for living room activities, only every time you come home unexpectedly, she jumps up like the house is on fire." He pressed his hands together in front of his chest. "I am begging you, Kyle. Do not screw this up for me. If you're coming home early, just shoot me a text. Set off fireworks in front of the house, throw a brick through the front window, send a freaking telegram. Heck, you can even call me—just please, please stop interrupting. Please."

Kyle's hard gaze adjusted by degrees into understanding. "You're in love with her."

Daniel massaged his temples, trying hard to keep his temper. "That's your opinion, and you're welcome to it, but what does that have to do with what I just said?"

"Nothing." He spun his keys on one finger. "It's just interesting. I thought I'd mention it in case you didn't know. And you definitely are." Kyle turned and opened his bedroom door.

"Hey, Kyle?" His brother turned in time to catch a pair of smelly socks against his face. "You're a jerk."

Kyle smirked and threw them back. "Fine. I'll try to communicate if I'm coming home early . . . as soon as you actually pay your rent." He closed his door.

"You just keep an eye on your PayPal account, then!" Daniel called through the closed door as he started down the stairs. "It's gonna be so full, the IRS will think you're laundering money!"

Kyle's door opened again. "Good, maybe it'll make up for the heating bill. I know you turned up the thermostat again! It's downright equatorial in here!"

With a sigh, Daniel took the stairs two at a time and landed at the bottom with a thump. Both chairs were empty. "Winnie?"

"In here," she called from the kitchen. He came through the doorway just in time to watch her bend over and put the bread in the oven, and he suddenly felt bad that he'd made fun of Kyle for watching Ainsley. Turned out, it was a pretty great pastime when it was attached to someone you really cared about. *You're in love with her.* Crazy. He just thought she was classy and gorgeous and brave and intelligent and wanted to make her laugh and take her to bed and give her presents that made her eyes light up and die for her if necessary.

"Daniel?" He could feel his face twisting with the realization that he was definitely in love, but he couldn't stop it. Winnie came over to him, oven mitts still on her hands, and rubbed his upper arms. "Are you okay? You look like you might pass out."

"No, no, I'm okay. Here, let me do that, I'm supposed to be doing things for you, not the other way around."

"I don't mind. It was better than sitting alone while you yelled at your brother."

"That wasn't yelling. And siblings are a blessing you should be glad you never got."

"I enjoy your siblings, actually. The ones I've met, anyway."

He blinked. "Would you like to meet more of them?"

"Yes, actually." She smiled. "Does that surprise you?"

"Yes. But I have no idea why. I guess I've never thought about bringing someone home before . . ." He gathered her in his arms, still staring down at her. "But you seem like the perfect person to start with."

"I was voted least likely to be intimidated in high school." She frowned. "They clearly didn't know about my relationship with my mother. Or Ethan. Okay, so they really didn't know me at all."

Daniel kissed her. "But you do give off an authoritative vibe. I noticed it right away. It's hot."

Winnie giggled. "Is it? Then I say let's go finish our dinner before the butter congeals again . . ."

"Yes, ma'am." They went back to the table, and much to his own disappointment, he couldn't think of another reason for her to sit on his lap again. Regardless, this night was back on track. His hopes were officially up. This would be the first of many.

CHAPTER
TWENTY-ONE

ON TUESDAY NIGHT, WINNIE was roasting red peppers in the oven for her spaghetti. It wasn't as much fun as over the open flame of the gas burners at her mom's house. She didn't want to admit it, but she was melancholy over the whole thing. Even when she didn't see her, they usually at least texted every few days. As it was, she'd heard nothing from her in ten days, and their interactions at work had been clinical and cold. Winnie hadn't seen her at all the last few days.

Someone knocked at the front door. Surprised, she wiped her oily hands on her blue denim apron and went to answer it. She peeked through the peephole: it was a man she didn't know. His shoulders were tight, and he was looking around as if he didn't want anyone to see him here. *Strange.* His hair was auburn and neatly gelled into place, his eyebrows thick; he wore a light beard that looked neat and intentional. He was well-dressed in a tailored black suit, his lavender tie perfectly complementing the rest of the outfit. But she didn't know him, and it wasn't her habit to answer the door to strange men while she was alone, so she went back to the kitchen. Another knock came.

"Starla?" the man called. "Baby, I'm sorry, I'm so sorry. This is just a misunderstanding, nothing happened. Open the door. Please."

That had Winnie marching back to the front door, wishing she had boots on. The effect of her bare feet stomping against the thin carpet was very unsatisfying.

The man seemed startled to see her.

"You must be Charlie."

"Yeah," he said, rubbing his hands together slowly. "Is Starla here?"

"I'm afraid not. Can I help you with something?"

"Well, I was just looking for Starla," he repeated, still looking around. "Who are you?" He craned his neck a little, clearly trying to get a better look inside.

"I'm Winifred Baker. This is my apartment." She leaned her hip against the doorframe, her arms crossed.

"Oh," he said, his face breaking into a slow smile. "Star mentioned Ainsley had a new roommate, but I hadn't had the pleasure yet. Hope you don't mind her coming around with the kids all the time. I'm Charlie Miller; I own Miller's Chevy dealership in Aumsville, me and my brother Jason." He stuck out his hand. Winnie did not move. *Wait, Jason and Lacey's baby is also Starla's niece? Wait, Jason, sweet, distractible, supportive Jason is related to Starla's crappy husband? How did I not put that together?* These small-town family trees were complicated sometimes.

"Mr. Miller, your wife isn't here, but she and your children are always welcome. I encourage you to keep looking for her. I'm sure she deserves whatever apology you were about to make, and then some."

His mouth was still hanging open when she shut the door. Ten minutes later, someone knocked again. She thought she'd heard him stomping down the stairs, but she'd turned up the music after she'd excused him, so perhaps she'd heard wrong. She peeked through the peephole again.

Mom. Without thinking about it, she whipped open the door. "Mom," she croaked.

"Winifred." Her voice was crisp, but her eyes were rimmed with red. "May I come in?"

"Of course." After her mother stepped inside, she poked her head out, and sure enough, there was Charlie, sitting in his silver Tahoe, talking on his phone. How long was he going to wait out there? Did he still think Starla was here? She pushed those questions aside for the moment as she shut the door. Her mother stood in her living room, back straight, holding her purse like it was a trigger to a bomb she was keeping from going off.

"Let me just . . ." Winnie hurried to the kitchen and took out the peppers, which were beautifully black. At least they were hard to mess up; they needed to cool before she could remove the skins, anyway. "Would you like to sit down?"

Sandra sat in a wooden kitchen chair, her legs together, her shoes still on, still clenching her purse. "I've taken some time to think; that's why I was away from work."

"I thought you were sick."

"Well, I had to save face somehow." She sighed. "I'm not happy about it, but after a lot of soul searching, I realize that this was my dream for you. I see now that I was wrong to pressure you. I should let you choose your own way."

"And?"

"I hear you that medical school is not in your future. I should have realized that I was pushing you too hard, that you could've passed the MCATs in your sleep . . . It never did exactly make sense."

For once, Winnie didn't wince. She didn't look at her shoes. She just stared at her mother and let her hurt show as the tears started falling.

"Did you tell Ethan that I wasn't an adult? Did you tell him to give me another chance?"

Her mother looked aghast. "No. I barely spoke to him when he called; he asked if you were retaking the MCATs, and I said I thought so. He wasn't right for you at all, no offense."

"I thought you loved him. You two were always exchanging books and news articles."

Her mother raised an eyebrow. "He was important to you. I was being polite. He occasionally had interesting thoughts on current events . . . but no. He wasn't my image of an ideal mate for you."

"Oh." This was going better than Winnie could've possibly projected, and she hadn't even needed Daniel's intervention. She pulled out her phone to text and find out where he was when her mother paused at the door.

"There was one other thing . . ."

"Yes?"

"On the subject of boyfriends, I did see you leaving the hospital with Daniel Durand the other day, looking very cozy. Make sure you keep your distance there."

"Keep my distance? Why?"

"Oh, Winifred." She was shaking her head. "How could you get involved with him? How could you think this was a good idea?"

"It's not like there's a waiting list of people interested, Mom. I'm over thirty. And honestly? I really like Daniel. And he really likes me."

Sandra scoffed. "Don't kid yourself, Winifred. He's young. This is a passing fad for him. I've heard people around the hospital talk; he's constantly on the prowl. He's very popular with a certain class of women."

"And what class is that, Mother?"

"Women who aren't interested in relationships."

"So you think he just wants to have sex with me?"

She sniffed. "Well, I wouldn't put it so bluntly, but yes, I do."

"So how long would you give it before the relationship flames out without sex?"

"Eight weeks."

"Deal."

Sandra scowled. "I beg your pardon?"

"I'll take your bet. I won't have sex with Daniel. I won't even kiss him, if you think it'll make a difference. And if we're still together in eight weeks, then you withdraw your objections. Do we have a deal?"

Her mother tipped her head, scrutinizing her carefully. "No sexual intimacy of any kind? Because there are other things that—"

"Mom." Winnie resisted the urge to cover her ears rather than listen to her mother clinically describe various types of outercourse. "No, no intimacy of any kind. I swear." She held out her right hand.

"You can still kiss him," she said, giving her a firm handshake. "Though I don't recommend it if you want to win."

"We're not teenagers, Mom. We can control ourselves."

"You may be able to. I have my doubts about him."

"Would you like to stay for dinner?"

"Sadly, I have a previous engagement."

"A previous engagement that doesn't involve a TV dinner and a stuffy literary work?"

"There's no need for that tone, Winifred."

Winnie laughed as her mom stood. "Oh, Mom. I missed you." She pulled her mom into a hug, her Chanel perfume covering the faint scent of disinfectant that always lingered on her. Sandra embraced her back, and Winnie heard the sniffle that indicated tears.

"I missed you, too, Winnie."

Her mother stayed and chatted just a few more minutes as she peeled the peppers and finished the spaghetti sauce simmering on the stove. She rushed to change her clothes a few minutes before Daniel was due to arrive, but pulled up short in front of her closet. She'd planned to wear her moss-green cabled sweater and her charcoal-gray pleated skirt . . . but maybe she shouldn't dress up so much, when she had to be the bearer of bad news. Hearing a knock, she quickly pulled on a pair of jeans and a pale-pink shirt that said "basic" that she'd used to paint her bedroom a few years ago.

He laughed when she opened the door. "What are you wearing?"

"It's casual. I'm casual sometimes."

He raised an eyebrow at her as he came in for a kiss. "Not that I've observed . . ."

"Let's eat." She still needed to figure out what she was going to say. But there was time. There was time as they passed the Caesar salad and the garlic bread. There was time as he poured her another glass of white. There was time as he washed her dishes (only fair, he said, since she'd cooked—Lord, she liked him), and still a little bit of time as he tugged her over to the couch. She could see the giant clock over the TV, taunting her with every tick as the evening wore on.

But it was time. She broke their kiss as gently as she could.

"So," Winnie started. "I may have done something kind of stupid."

Daniel leaned back. "You? Stupid? That doesn't compute."

She chuckled nervously. "Well, maybe wait until I've explained . . . I made a deal with my mother."

He sat up into his own space, shaking his head. "Wait, you guys are talking again? Win, that's great."

"It is great, it's really great. She apologized for pressuring me, and she's going to try to accept that this is what I want to do with my life."

He stroked her leg innocently, but it derailed her thoughts nonetheless. "A deal? What kind of deal?"

"Well, a bet, really."

"That doesn't sound better . . ." He crossed his arms. "And this affects me somehow? What did you wager?"

She grimaced, pulling her lips to the side. "First of all, I actually think this could be a good thing, in the long run, because we weren't really friends before we started seeing each other, so we don't have the long history that—"

"Fred. Just tell me. I'm not going to be mad." Given that he already seemed a little bit mad, she wasn't sure she should really believe that.

"This will give us time to get to know each other really well, be really in tune with each other, and build that solid foundation for our relationship . . ."

His confused glare told her it was time to just say it, and she sighed.

"I told her we wouldn't have sex for eight weeks." Winnie pulled her T-shirt up over her mouth, burying her face in her clothes as if she could hide from the consequences of her actions. Daniel's jaw went slack. He stared at her, searching her face as if looking for any hint that she was joking. When he found none, he took a deep breath.

"I'm just going to step into the bathroom for a moment."

"Daniel, I . . ." She moved to go after him, but he held up one finger, and the flaring of his nostrils convinced her to just give him what he'd asked for. He stepped quietly into the bathroom and closed the door behind him. Winnie heard a soft thump-thump-thump, and she guessed he was hitting his head against the wall.

She was bending her fingers back, biting her lip, when he came back.

"Daniel, it was stupid, I know—"

Holding up a finger, he went to the kitchen and poured himself a glass of orange juice. He chugged the whole thing, then set the glass down carefully by the sink.

"Why . . . why would you promise her that? It's none of her business what we do together."

"That's true, it isn't her business. But she started talking about you and how you're not serious about any of the women you date and how you'd get bored with me . . ."

Daniel's gaze hardened at that, but Winnie didn't stop.

"I told her," she murmured, "that we were serious about each other. That it was more than just physical. That it was more than a fling. Was I wrong?"

"No," he said, taking her face between his hands. "Hell no. I'm as serious as preeclampsia about you."

"Sweetheart, I told you to stop with the medical similes. It's just weird."

"But . . ." His eyes told her he was holding something back, afraid to say it aloud. "Do you . . . I mean, it's not that you don't want to, right?"

"No," Winnie said sharply, mirroring his hold, needing to be closer.

"Because if you don't want to, I'm not going to pressure you."

"Daniel, I do want to. I want to so much, I am all the wanting. I swear."

He brought their foreheads together, and it was the most pained smile she'd ever seen him give her. More forced even than when Mrs. Foster ran over his toe with her wheelchair. "At least I can still kiss you." He pulled back to see her better. "I *can* still kiss you, right?"

"Yes." She gave him a lingering peck, just for emphasis. "Definitely. In fact, she seemed to encourage that."

"Yeah, she wants us to fail."

"That's very possible." She kissed him again. "But we're not going to."

"Nope."

A thought occurred to Winnie. "Not that she'd really know . . ."

Daniel pressed his lips into a flat line. "Fred, when I make a bet, I keep my end. I once had a game of Monopoly running with Philip and Kyle for two months because no one would concede defeat. My mother finally confiscated the game just as I was about to pull off my epic victory. We can do this." He kissed her. "We're in this together, right?"

"Yes, absolutely. We're a team."

"Good. And you're not mad?"

"Oh, no, I am mad."

She covered her face. "I'm sorry. She's a bit of an arrogant jerk, but she's my mom, and I love her, and it's been weird being on the outs with her. I kind of played all my cards on the 'I'm not going to medical school' thing. I just wanted—"

"Hey." He pulled her hands down. "It's okay. I wish you'd talked to me first, but we'll figure it out." Daniel pulled her into a tight hug, and as she felt his chest rise and fall, she hoped like crazy that he was right.

CHAPTER TWENTY-TWO

DANIEL HAD JUST FINISHED a percutaneous nephrostomy for Mr. Townsend and his kidney stones, wincing the whole time. It had been a good experience, but delicate procedures like that made him nervous, which in turn made him hungry. He had just collapsed on the lumpy futon in the on-call room and taken an enormous bite of an onion bagel when Dr. Trout found him.

"Dr. Baker says you have to go home."

Daniel sat up. "Why?" Surely she wasn't going to take her frustration out on him at work?

"She said you're up against your time limits."

"Really?" Daniel thought he should've had two hours left for the week, and he also knew they were short-staffed today. The Libby Zion law prohibited interns and residents from working the long hours they'd been forced into in the past, but he really hated leaving when people needed his help. That was one reason he'd already decided to stay in Timber Falls; he wanted to be where he was needed. He felt a pang of annoyance that she was avoiding him by sending Greg. They were both adults—they could work this out.

"She also said you should keep track of your own hours, because the hospital doesn't need the liability." Greg grimaced as he slowly pulled his head out of the way of the closing door. "Just the messenger, don't shoot me."

Grunting, Daniel got to his feet and grabbed his backpack. It was lunchtime; she'd probably be in the cafeteria. He wasn't going to confront her, just talk things over. As he expected, she was eating with Dr. Udawatte. She'd taken Tharushi under her wing a little more than him and Dr. Trout, partly because they were both women, he expected. Then again, he'd never really tried to get more into Dr. Baker's good graces; he'd never had a reason to. Until now.

He approached the orange table cautiously; only Tharushi had noticed his arrival. "May I join you?"

Dr. Baker turned. Her face registered mild surprise, then she nodded. "As I was saying, they're still examining exactly what makes their oral bacteria different and how it's related to heart health, but it's an interesting correlation."

Tharushi nodded, her wavy black hair bobbing. "I hope they can isolate it. So much research could be done at the microbiotic level. I can't wait until there are more tests available. It's less invasive and inexpensive."

"And yet, our textbooks barely mention that kind of diagnostic information," Daniel added. "Hard to keep them up to date when medicine changes so quickly."

Dr. Baker took a sip of her water. "I thought I sent you home."

"Uh, yes. You did, I'm on my way." He cleared his throat. "I just wanted to clear the air before I left."

"Oh?" Her gaze was disinterested.

"First of all, I did have two hours left by my count, and I'm happy to stay and serve those."

"Unnecessary."

"And secondly, I just wanted to say that I really like your daughter and have good intentions where she's concerned. I hope that'll become obvious over the course of the next few weeks."

"Why?" Tharushi asked, perking up. "What happens in a few weeks?"

"Nothing," Daniel muttered, glaring at her to let it go. They were fairly close; she wouldn't take it the wrong way. But she was the wrong person to be sending silent messages to at that moment.

"I've made a wager with my daughter that if they don't have sexual intercourse, he'll become disinterested in her within two months."

Daniel froze. *Did she really just air our personal stuff to my colleague?* Disbelief quickly ceded space in his brain to anger. Blinding, paralyzing anger.

"What did you wager?" Tharushi asked, her eyes wide, her gaze ping-ponging between them.

"My acceptance," Sandra replied, with the air of a queen explaining to a peasant why he shouldn't mind paying exorbitant taxes on his crops.

"Your *acceptance* is irrelevant," Daniel snapped. Dr. Baker pivoted toward him slowly, and Daniel knew he had made an elephant-sized mistake. Maybe even Hulk-sized.

"Long hours will take a toll on your judgment," she said quietly. "That's why the eighty-hour law is in place. Go home, Dr. Durand."

She turned back to her conversation with Tharushi, and he stood slowly and pushed in his chair. He knew the smart thing to do would be to just walk away . . . but this was too important.

"I'm in love with your daughter."

He must've said it loudly—either that or the other people in the cafeteria were uniquely tuned into the frequency of gossip, because twenty heads turned his way, including Sandra's.

He felt his face getting hot, but he plowed on. "I love Winnie, and I'll prove it. To both of you." Daniel blasted through the cafeteria without looking back, but he heard the whispers starting before he was through the double doors. People were so immature sometimes. He slammed the door of his Volvo and started driving home. It was one, and traffic was terrible. That is to say, there were other cars on the road with him all the way back to Timber Falls. He stopped at the Subway to pick up dinner, and by the time he'd claimed his foot-long meatball sub, his brother had texted him.

Kyle: I didn't think public declarations of love were your thing.

Daniel: They're not.

Kyle: That's not what Tharushi said.

Daniel: Leave me alone.

Kyle: When's the wedding?

Kyle: Is Ainsley going to be your best man?

Daniel: First of all, jerkface, you'd be my best man, and you know it.

Daniel: Second of all, jerkface, I said leave me alone.

Kyle: Dad and I are going up to Olallie tomorrow to try for some yellow perch. You in?

He sighed. He might as well go. He hated people gossiping about him; getting a little out of town might be a good idea.

Daniel: Not too early, though.

Kyle: Can't go early this time of year anyway.

Kyle: Which you'd know if you were any kind of fisherman.

Daniel sent him a gif of a guy fishing, getting pulled into the ocean. Sighing, he went back to his car.

"I FEEL LIKE THIS IS the setup of a joke," Daniel said, climbing into the metal rowboat and carefully making his way to the bow. "Three doctors get into a boat in the middle of winter . . ."

"The joke will be if we catch anything," Kyle muttered.

"Hey. Optimism, please. Your old dad's been around this lake a time or two."

"Then why isn't it called catching?" Daniel asked, grinning. Evan glared at him as he passed him the tackle box and green nylon net. They headed down the edge of the lake, the slow *pull, pull, pull* of his father's strokes of the oars jerking Daniel's head forward.

"Heard a thing . . . ," Evan said, and Daniel pivoted to face him.

"Yeah?"

"Yeah. Heard you had a boom box held above your head in the cafeteria. Red rose between your teeth or something . . ."

Daniel rolled his eyes so hard, it was physically painful. "Yeah, I came out here to forget about my personal problems, so . . ."

"I don't think of love as a problem. Don't you want to be with Winnie?" Dad asked.

Daniel hesitated. "Of course I do. It's just never been this much *work* before."

"From what I hear, most relationships are," Kyle replied, flipping open the tackle box to retrieve the foam cup of worms.

"And I hate having the whole town in our business."

"Yeah, that was shrewd on Dr. Baker's part," Kyle said, baiting Daniel's hook. "No offense, but you've always been a little . . ."

"A little what?"

"Not a lot, just a little bit . . ."

"Say it, jerkface."

"Shallow. You're shallow, mostly when it comes to women. But a little when it comes to your personal care routine as well. No man should own so many hair products."

"I am not shallow!" he shouted, standing up suddenly. The boat rocked wildly, and all three of them grabbed for the side. He didn't want to get wet; he loved this shirt.

Oh.

Maybe that's what his brother was talking about. But that was vanity, not shallowness.

"Fine, you can bait your own hook next time," Kyle said, and Daniel shuddered. He didn't mind catching the fish or even cleaning them, but he hated the way the worms writhed when he tried to spear them.

His dad adjusted his baseball hat. "How would you feel if we disapproved of Winnie?"

"Why would you disapprove of Winnie? Winnie is amazing. Winnie is the best."

"Well, Mom's never met her. Perhaps she'd disapprove of her nails." The younger men snickered. Their mother was even more vain than Daniel. "Would it be fair of her to ask you to cut your mom out of your life?"

"I'm not suggesting that her mom not be part of her life, I just . . . She's an adult. I'm an adult. I just don't think I need her approval."

"No, you don't. But you should want it."

"If Winnie approves, that should be enough. Kyle, back me up."

"No. You're wrong. Sorry."

Daniel sighed and set down his pole between his feet, resting his forearms on his knees. "Fine. Why should I want her approval?"

"Because that parent loves her child more than you can possibly imagine. She's raised her alone, worked at our dinky little hospital when she could be doing bigger and better things, in order for Winnie to be near her grandparents, for her to have a family." Evan brought the oars back slowly, letting the boat coast for a moment as they dripped, casting ripples. "She is all her hopes and dreams, the last vestige of the one great romance of her life. And you should want the person who loves her best to think you're the best person to love her when she's gone."

Daniel let his head drop, feeling the stretch of his muscles down his back, feeling the reality of what his dad had just proclaimed on his shoulders like a weight. He wanted to be that person for her, the person she could depend on. But it was going to take more, more than he'd been willing to give to relationships up until now.

"Damn," said Kyle, breaking the silence. "That's downright eloquent, Dad."

"You want to go swimming?"

Kyle smirked. "No, sir."

"That's what I thought." He glanced at his youngest son. "That being said, some people are unreasonable. If she just won't approve, you and Winnie will have to decide where to go from there. It's your life. If you want to live it together, you should, but it may be a bigger sacrifice than she's willing to make."

Daniel was quiet a moment longer. "So you're saying I should respect Dr. Baker's role in her life, even if I think she's wrong."

"Exactly. Respect that you both love Winnie and want what's best for her, even if you don't see eye to eye." He pulled out a paleo granola bar. "And then go mow her lawn for her."

"I think she employs a company to do that . . ."

"You can always come do mine."

"Do you remember residency, like, at all?"

"Son, do I ever." His dad grinned. "I'd just met this cute beautician, and all I wanted was to feel her run her long fingernails through my hair . . ." Both brothers talked over him to drown out the story they'd heard too many times already. The conversation turned to medicine, which turned to his father and brother quizzing him. They returned to shore two hours later, short on snacks, long on cold. His dad's phone rang as they were tying the boat back to the dock.

"Your phone works here?" Daniel asked, pulling out his own: no signal.

His dad ignored him. "Hi, sweetheart." He paused. "Yes, I'll ask them. You boys want to come for dinner?"

"Me," said Kyle, gathering life jackets.

"Not me," said Daniel. He wanted to talk to Winnie first; she should be off today.

"Just the big one," his dad said into the phone. "Yes, we had a great time." He listened for a moment. "Oh, none, but that doesn't matter."

CHAPTER
TWENTY-THREE

HE'D HAD NO CELL RECEPTION at Olallie Lake, so Daniel checked his messages on the way down. Apparently, the town had been busy.

"Daniel." Winnie's voice on his voicemail was tense. Also, who still left voicemails? She was so adorable. "Someone in the mini mart just asked if I'm Team Daniel or Team Sandra." She sighed shakily, and he hoped like heck she wasn't crying. Not over this. Small towns, this is what they did. It was an act of love, really. "This is officially getting out of hand. We need to do something. Call me back."

"The town is drawing battle lines," Daniel informed them as his dad pulled off the highway into town.

"Put me down for Team Daniel," his dad said.

"Me too," Kyle grunted. "Baker clearly doesn't know who she's up against."

"I kinda figured, but good to have that confirmed." Daniel smirked. Normally, the hubbub would all blow over in a few days, but this was an eight-week bet. There would be a town meeting on Friday: that was quite a while to wait. He'd need to employ desperate measures. "Can you drop me at Hattie's?"

"Ooh. He's pulling out the big guns."

"Better bring something good," Kyle muttered.

"Shoot, you're right. Drop me at home; I've got some baking to do."

NINETY MINUTES LATER, he was walking up the steps of the blue and white farmhouse with winter-blooming camellias flanking the stairway, the still-cooling brownies wrapped in a thick terry cloth towel balanced on his hip. They weren't frosted, but they'd have to do. He'd also brought carrots for Sir Patrick Stewart and Dame Maggie Smith, her American quarter horses. The front door opened, then the screen door, and Hattie Meyer-Bagsby was grinning at him, hands on her hips where her brown corduroy pants met her paisley polyester blouse.

"I wondered when you'd show up here."

He grinned back. "How are you, Hattie?"

"Fine, just fine. Come on in and tell me what's on your mind."

Daniel wiped his feet carefully on her welcome mat, which read "No soliciting, unless you've got cookies." The town council was in charge of Timber Falls, officially. They conducted town meetings, made sure the sanitation people picked up the trash, and arbitrated disputes. But Hattie . . . Hattie ran Timber Falls in actuality. The high school was named for Colton D. Meyer, her great-grandfather and one of the founding members of the town. Her family still owned the commercial timber company that employed half the population—Ainsley's mom, Nancy, included. Her entryway was full of photographs, just above the natural bead board paneling: candid pictures of her late husband, Davis; childhood pictures of her kids, Francine and Forest, both in their forties now; faded black-and-white pictures of the town in the twenties, when the mill was first built.

"Brought you something," he said, passing her the pan, careful not to let the metal touch her skin. Daniel sat down at her kitchen table. She had an office, but she seldom conducted business there anymore.

"Aren't you thoughtful?" She smiled, even though they both knew it hadn't been optional. Her favors were easily bought, but they did come at a price. "Want some tea?"

"Yes, please."

She put her blue Le Creuset kettle on the back burner and lit it with a match. "You want to know what team I'm on, or you want me to shut it down?"

He drummed his fingers on the table. "I don't know. Originally, I just wanted you to shut it down . . . but now you've got me curious."

Hattie cut herself a brownie, sniffed it delicately, and took a small bite. "Ghirardelli mix?"

He nodded, smiling.

"You've got good taste. These are better than homemade."

"You're the connoisseur." She took a larger bite and sat down next to him, chewing.

"I like hearing you use those ten-dollar words. I remember your mom sharing prayer requests, worried you weren't going to pass third grade, then fourth, then fifth. I told her she had nothing to fear at the time, and you know, I find I like being right." Hattie was in her late sixties, and her health had been good since a cancer scare three years ago. "You like this girl?" He wanted to correct her that Winnie was a woman, not a girl, but he knew she meant no harm by it.

"I do. Very much."

"I'd like to have a new midwife around permanently. Frances Mitton isn't going to be working forever."

"Well, I'm glad my love life serves your purposes, Mrs. Meyer-Bagsby." He grinned when she raised an eyebrow at his sass, not regretting it at all. His grandparents were all dead; Hattie was the closest thing he had now. "Are you going to keep me guessing?"

"Pardon?"

"Don't 'pardon' me like you're senile; that gray hair doesn't fool me. You haven't told me what team you're on."

"Yours, of course. How can you even ask me?" She pushed the pan of brownies toward him, and he took one for himself. "How does your girl feel about the publicity?"

"She's not crazy about it. She's from—" He started to say California, but he stopped himself just in time. "Salem. They're not so all up in each other's business there, I don't think."

"Mmm." She dusted the chocolate off her hands and got up to pour her tea from the steaming kettle. "Well, I can have them tone things down if you want, but it's not going to stop people from talking. They'll just be less public about it."

"I think that'd still be for the best. Thanks, Hattie."

"If she's going to be one of us, though, she's going to have to get used to it . . ."

"Yeah." He had the urge to scrub his scalp with his fingers, but he didn't want to mess up his hair. *Shallow.*

"You want some advice?"

"Please."

"There's an all-church work day at St. Thomas Episcopalian Church, where her mother attends, next Saturday. Put it on your calendar."

He pulled out his phone to leave himself an audio message.

"And the PTO is having a pancake fundraiser for the high school's new pool. See if you can get on the serving line."

"This is good stuff," he muttered, opting to type it so she wouldn't stop talking. "Anything else?"

Hattie shrugged and sat back. "Just that you get in front of her outside of work as much as possible and be your charming self." She pointed at him sternly. "And do things that'll keep you out of the house, to avoid temptation. My team's gonna win this thing."

He paused. "What if I screw this up?"

"You won't."

"But if I do, everyone's going to know we failed. They're going to know Dr. Baker won."

"So what?" she asked. "People will forget about it as soon as Jean Helsing and James Miller get into a shouting match about the gravel truck's route the next time it snows."

Daniel nodded, chuckling. "You're probably right. Thanks. I've gotta go see Winnie now."

"You want to take some of the brownies? Might help smooth things over."

He smiled gently. "No, I'm good; she's more of an ice cream person. Those are yours. And the carrots are for your royalty out back."

"They'll appreciate them, I'm sure."

"See you, Hattie."

She walked him to the door. "Don't be such a stranger. And tell your teacher friend to ask out your brother, the grumpy one. I'm tired of waiting for him."

Daniel laughed. "Yes, ma'am." He had no such intention, he thought as he drove over to Ainsley and Winnie's apartment, nervous. He took the steps two at a time, and she had the door open already when he got to the top.

"Hey." Her tone was slightly cold; that was strange.

"Hey." He pulled her close and kissed her. She tasted like peppermint tea, and it felt appropriate, because peppermint tasted like Christmas, and that was how Winnie made him feel. Happy.

"You got my message?" She bit out the words, and he scowled.

"Yes, sorry. I was so busy working on the solution, I forgot to text you." He came into the apartment. Ainsley was sprawled on the couch on her stomach, eating popcorn and reading a thick novel. "Hey, Slick."

"Hey." She smiled. Hattie's request came to mind, and he bit back the words. They needed to work it out themselves. He shouldn't get involved, even though he'd love to see them together. Before he could say anything more to Ainsley, Winnie took his hand and started dragging him down the hall toward the bedrooms. His eyes wide, he looked to Ainsley for an explanation, who just smirked.

"I have twenty bucks riding on you two!" she called after them. "Leave room for the Holy Spirit!"

Winnie didn't slow down. She pulled Daniel past the bathroom, past Ainsley's room, and straight into her bedroom and shut the door. He hadn't been in here yet, and he took the opportunity to look around, even as his mind strained to figure out what was going on. Her modern, floral down comforter was on her neatly made bed, and on her windows were a coordinating gray roller shade and pink blackout curtains. Her shoes were paired, each inside its own little pocket, in a canvas shoe holder on the door of her closet; the clothes inside seemed to be organized by season, then color. Her bookcase was full of midwifery textbooks, comic books, and childhood favorites. The desk in the corner, however, was a mountain of papers and books, and he grinned to see that evidence of her imperfection. Though, strangely, he thought it made her a little more perfect.

"Hey!" She snapped her fingers near his eyes, and irritation bristled inside him. He focused on what she was shoving in his face: her phone.

Martina: Hear that?

Martina: That's the sound of hearts breaking all over Timber Falls tonight . . .

Martina: Because Daniel Durand just professed his love for you to the entire cafeteria.

Daniel blinked. "What's wrong?"

"What's wrong?" she repeated slowly, her voice dangerously low, heavy with disbelief. "What's wrong is that you told all our coworkers that you love me before you told *me*."

"Oh." He rubbed at his beard. "That was a mistake, huh?"

"You think?" Her fists were balled at her sides; she looked like she wanted to hit him. He didn't think it was too likely, but he'd never really fought with a girlfriend before. When things got ugly, he'd just leave. Not an option this time . . . Well, he'd better try to fix it immediately.

"I love you, Winnie."

She stomped a bare foot against the carpet. "Stop that," she said fiercely.

"Stop what?" he asked, hopelessly confused now.

"Stop being so sweet. I'm mad at you. I'm really, really mad at you."

He grinned, sidling up close to her. "I love you, Fred. I love you so much. I love you more than all the microbes in all the petri dishes in all the world."

"Don't," she said, her voice warbling. "Don't say it unless you mean it."

He moved close enough to whisper in her ear. "I love you more than all the hippies in the Northwest. I love you more than all the recycling centers, all the microbreweries, and all the marijuana put together."

"Now you're just being trite," she whispered back, and he chuckled.

"You're right. There's no appropriate metaphor for it. They all fall short." He caught her tear as it fell, wiping it from her cheek. "I'm sorry I didn't tell you first."

Winnie skipped the usual warm-up kissing; she caught the back of his head, bringing his lips to hers, dipping into his mouth with her soft tongue. He was so surprised, he ceded all control to her before he knew what was happening. His arms found their way around her, his hands roaming over her back, into her hair. Eyes closed, he reveled in her softness, in her curves, her closeness. They were a perfect union of heat and touch, kissing with synchronized give and take, like they'd been doing it for decades.

Until Winnie sunk her teeth into his bottom lip. It was like she'd flipped a switch, and that switch was his rational mind. Daniel reached down and picked her up, carrying her over to the bed. He tossed her onto it and covered her body with his. He devoured her with kisses, and based on her soft sighs and happy hums, he wasn't the only one thinking this was a great idea. But he did hear the toilet flush in the bathroom next door, and that reminded him that they weren't alone. Ainsley was here. Ainsley was Team Daniel, as were Hattie and Kyle and his dad. And Team Daniel was determined not to let this fail.

Desperately, he tried to slow them down; as determined as he'd been to be closer to her a moment ago, he now felt an equal determination to detour them from where they'd been heading. His heart rate started to slow as she followed his lead, relief flooding him. Daniel rolled off and lay next to her on the bed, breathing hard, and he reached for her hand.

"I love you, too, Daniel," she said, turning her face into his neck, her voice breathy, and it almost did him in. He covered his face with his arm and groaned, and he heard Winnie's low chuckle in answer. "That was close, wasn't it?"

"Fred, you have no idea."

CHAPTER
TWENTY-FOUR

THE SCENT OF MAPLE syrup, orange juice, and bacon surrounded Winnie like a fog. It permeated the gym. She and Daniel had agreed to work the pancake fundraiser event together, following Hattie's advice; she'd gotten people to stop with all the team talk. Except for the Durands; they were all still very vocally Team Daniel, or so she heard. His family seemed very sweet . . . She hoped she could fit in with them as well as she seemed to get along with Daniel. Their standard family dinner was at the same time as hers with her grandparents, unfortunately, so they hadn't gotten much time together yet.

"Good morning, Dr. Baker!" she greeted her mother cheerfully. Sandra was not a morning person, and it showed; she held a compostable coffee cup in a death grip, already downing it, along with a paper plate with pineapple, honeydew melon, and strawberries, and utensils. "Would you like some bacon?"

"I'm surprised to see you here," she commented to Daniel, who smiled politely, rubbing one eye under his glasses.

Winnie plopped two pieces of bacon on her plate unceremoniously and decided to answer the question for him. "Oh, I signed up ages ago; Ainsley twisted my arm. She promised me an easy job. Daniel wanted to tag along to spend some time to-gether. Right, babe?" ~

"Right," he said, shaking his head a little, as if it were fuzzy. He'd just gotten off a twenty-four-hour shift, which Dr. Baker would likely know, and Winnie had picked him up rather than let him drive like that. She knew how dead one felt after a long day at the hospital.

"Didn't you already donate toward the pool fund?" Winnie asked.

Her mother nodded. "But it's good to show up for things. Be seen."

Winnie disagreed; what was good on a Saturday morning was yoga, comic books, and time alone . . . or maybe hanging out with Daniel. "Being seen" didn't factor into her weekends. "Well, enjoy your fruit salad."

Her mother moved down the line, and at her elbow, Daniel silently yawned.

"You should go home. It's fine, really."

"No," he said through another yawn. "I'm here. I'm help-ing. I . . ."

She served the next person their two allotted pieces of thick bacon, then turned to him. She stared at him expectantly, waiting for him to finish his thought. He didn't.

"Daniel?"

He startled, then turned to her. She couldn't help but feel alarmed.

"Did you just fall asleep on your feet?"

"No . . . I don't think so. I'm not sure."

"All right, I'm taking you home."

"No, Win, you stay. I'll find someone else to . . ." He took off his plastic apron and stumbled away from the tables toward the locker rooms. She couldn't watch him to make sure he was okay, due to the heavy number of bacon lovers, but she did manage to see him disappear down the hall. In the gym, she saw her mother casually wind her way toward the town council's table; several of them were on the hospital's board, and she knew her mother was concerned about keeping their grants for the residency program.

An hour slipped by, awash in carbs. Ainsley touched her elbow.

"Gloria's going to take over for you up here," she said, gesturing to a petite Latina woman next to her, already aproned and gloved. Winnie stepped back.

"Oh, okay. But I should warn you, I don't have great cooking skills."

"Actually, there's a bit of a situation outside the bathrooms, and I was hoping you could help me resolve it."

"Oh?" Her mind snapped into work mode. "A medical situation?"

"No. Well, sort of. Just come on." Ainsley turned and strode between the bleachers into the dark hallway. She stopped by the drinking fountains and gestured to the man on the floor, clad in blue scrubs, still wearing his glasses, curled up under the metal bowls in the fetal position, his arms tucked under his head for a pillow. Daniel was out cold.

"Did you try to wake him up?"

"Everything short of throwing water on him or setting his scrubs on fire." She glanced around, then moved closer conspiratorially. "He's kind of freaking people out. Do you think you could take him home?"

"Yes . . . Do you think Kyle could help me get him into the car? Is he here?"

"No, Kyle doesn't come to this stuff, but I think his dad is here. Let me . . ." Her voice trailed off, and Winnie turned to see who she was staring at. Her mother stood, her white pea coat on, her Michael Kors purse hung on her right arm, about five feet away.

"Is he okay?"

"I think so, he was just very tired."

"Then why did he come?"

Winnie felt her anger rising, but Ainsley beat her to it.

"Oh, I don't know," her roommate snapped. "Maybe he was trying to prove to *someone unreasonable* that he really likes your daughter and wants to do things that are important to her. Do you think that's a possibility?"

Dr. Baker lifted her chin slightly, and her lips curved into a mild smile. "It's possible. But I certainly never intended for him to put his health at risk in order to do so."

"I'm going to go get Evan; excuse me." Ainsley stormed off, leaving mother and daughter to stare at the sleeping doctor on the floor. Without a word, her mother passed by them and went into the bathrooms, and Winnie sighed, massaging her temples.

Ainsley came back soon with Evan; he had dark hair like Kyle, with a little more silver mixed in, and the same dark eyes.

"So nice to finally meet you," he said, pulling her into a friendly hug. "I've heard so much about you from Daniel. Farrah wants you to come to dinner sometime soon." His manner was open and kind, and Winnie liked him immediately. "All right," he said, rubbing his hands together. "Let's get this young man to the car, shall we?"

Daniel never came fully awake as they supported him on either side, taking him out the back to avoid curious stares and concerned questioning.

"So, Winnie," he asked, grunting a little as they got him up onto the curb. "Do you like biking?"

"Well, I did as a kid. I haven't done it much lately." They managed to get the door open, and Daniel tumbled into the front seat.

"Thanks for your help," Winnie said, slightly out of breath from the exertion. "I'll make sure he gets into bed."

"Just don't climb in after; I'm Team Daniel," Evan joked, and Winnie felt a blush race over her chest and cheeks. Evan looked a little chagrined at her embarrassment, and he hurried on. "Sorry, bad joke. Do whatever you want, I just . . . I'm rooting for you guys, relationship-wise. Most of the girls he's dated would've left him sleeping under the water fountain." He rubbed his stubbled chin. "Then again, I don't think he would've shown up here for any of them." He gave her another quick side hug, and Winnie grinned, thinking this must be where Daniel got his touchy way with people. The paternal affection was very welcome; he reminded her of her grandpa. They'd probably get along famously.

She climbed into the car. Daniel was asleep again. Sighing, she rolled down the windows. It started to rain on the way home—just a sprinkle, but it had Daniel looking around in confusion.

"I'm wet," he said, rubbing his arms. "I'm cold."

"Welcome back to the land of the living, dear. I'm taking you home, and the windows are open so you stay awake long enough to get you into the house . . ."

He sighed heavily. "Okay." He turned his head to snuggle more deeply into the seat, and he was asleep again before she turned onto his street, dampness apparently irrelevant.

CHAPTER
TWENTY-FIVE

DANIEL WAS STILL YAWNING as Dr. Baker passed out their information packets the next Monday morning; he'd been getting up early to have breakfast with Winnie since he was gone at night. He'd caught up a little over the weekend, but overall, the missed sleep was taking its toll. Dr. Baker liked to do these study guides based on the cases they'd seen the previous week, and then give them a quiz. It was above and beyond, but it didn't hurt to have more reinforcement of the material. He just wished it wasn't printed; if he could get it digitally, he could have a program read it to him. He scratched his belly absentmindedly, and his gaze fell to the table. His paper looked different. Did his prescription need to be adjusted again?

Picking up the packet, he looked at it more carefully. It wasn't as hard to read as usual. She'd printed it in Open Dyslexic, the font he'd used for most of his papers in college, which he'd change to Times New Roman before he turned them in. At the top, she'd handwritten a note that was more difficult to read, despite being in neat, uniformly slanted cursive:

I apologize for not doing this sooner. Please let me know if there's anything else I can do to accommodate your learning needs.
–Dr. Sandra Baker

Daniel smiled, then looked up to see that she was watching him as the other residents and interns chatted quietly, and he gave her a nod of thanks. *Is she finally coming around? Did falling asleep at a pancake breakfast really turn things in my favor?*

"Today we're going to discuss myocardial infarction, as the symptoms are quite different for women than for men and are often mistaken for panic attacks. Dr. Durand, what are the symptoms of myocardial infarction for men?"

"Pain in the left arm, discomfort behind the breastbone. Shortness of breath, nausea, sweating."

"And for women?"

His mind raced. He could hear the podcast he'd listened to, still in his head. "They're less likely to include chest pain and more likely to happen during rest than exertion."

"Good. Dr. Trout, what else?"

"Women are more likely to have pain outside of the chest, and to experience feeling faint, a cold sweat."

"Dr. Udawatte?"

"Severe inability to sleep, pale or clammy skin."

She set down her papers quietly. "I'm glad you're all so up to speed on this. Can you explain to me, then, why none of you caught the two heart attacks that Mrs. Graves had over the weekend? Dr. Harper from Cardiology was just here after Nurse Lopez realized that her stomach pain and sleeplessness were due to more than just the cafeteria food. Mrs. Graves had a myocardial infarction on Friday night and Saturday morning, based on her echocardiogram. She's being taken into surgery this afternoon." Daniel's own heart clenched; he'd prescribed her a sleeping pill Friday night, but they'd all been in there with her, discussing the case on rounds. They thought she had the flu; Tharushi had helped her to the toilet when she felt like she was going to pass out. They thought she was just dehydrated.

"You all owe Nurse Lopez a debt of gratitude. Know the symptoms. Did any of you touch her hands, her feet? Did you look at her health history? Her mother died of a heart attack around the same age. You must be more thorough. Look at everything. Assume nothing."

They all nodded, and the mood was somber. After they discussed the new cases and did their rounds, Dr. Baker excused them to tackle the various tasks they'd been assigned. Daniel's list was long today; it took him three hours to make a dent in it. His stomach growled; it had been a long time since his 5:30 a.m. breakfast with Winnie. They'd eaten on the couch despite her general objection to the activity, snuggled together, her in her pajamas. It was the best part of his day.

But this part, this was the worst. Or at least, he hoped it would be the worst. Every patient he interacted with now, he felt his paranoia growing that he was missing something. That some obvious piece of the puzzle was eluding him. He should have been eating lunch, but he couldn't stop thinking about Mrs. Graves . . . After two bites of his salami sandwich, he put it back in the fridge and went down to Cardiology. His pager went off just as he knocked at Mrs. Graves's door: *Come to the ER for an intake.* They'd just have to wait a few minutes. At her voice, Daniel opened the door of her room quietly.

"Dr. Durand. I didn't think they let interns down here," she said with a grin. He'd known her for more than twenty years; her husband was his mailman. She had a weekly appointment with his mom to get her toenails painted.

"They probably shouldn't," he said softly, trying to grin back, but it felt like lifting a hundred pounds. "Mrs. Graves, I just wanted to apologize—"

Someone knocked on the door, and it opened before either of them could say anything.

"There you are," said Dr. Baker. "You're needed in the ER."

"Yes, I'll be right there." He swallowed hard, frustrated that he'd now have an audience for what he wanted to say. He lowered his voice. "Mrs. Graves, I'm so sorry I didn't catch what was happening to you over the weekend. How are you feeling? Have they talked through the surgery with you?"

"Oh yes, Dr. Harper just explained everything. And don't worry about it, dear: it could happen to anyone. You weren't the only one who missed it."

"No, but I'm still sorry. Our team should've caught it sooner." He patted her hand gently, avoiding where the IV was attached to the back of it. "I'll come see you afterwards, all right? I'll bring Jell-O."

"I like the strawberry ones. Don't get a cherry by mistake. It tastes like cough medicine."

"Yes, ma'am." He smiled. "Best of luck. See you later."

"Of course you will."

He turned to leave and was surprised to see Dr. Baker still standing in the doorway, watching him, pressing a chart to her chest. She followed him down the hallway.

"You need to be careful," she said.

"I know, I screwed up the diagnosis with the sleeping pill."

"Not that. Admitting your mistake. You don't want the patient to be able to come back with a malpractice suit."

He stopped walking, and she stopped, too. He glared at her for a long moment, debating about what to say before he took a deep breath.

"With all due respect, she already knows we made a mistake. It doesn't hurt to apologize. I'd rather have a patient who trusts me to be straight with her than one who's wondering what I'm trying to hide." He strode away before she could answer, knowing that he was pushing the boundaries of professionalism by calling her out. But that's who he was: integrity mattered. That's how his dad and his brother were, too. He knew it wasn't just him.

He made it down to the ER quickly and processed the patient into the hospital. He took longer than necessary to check him over: four-year-old male, high fever, bright-red patch rash on his face and body. Daniel started with his hands and feet, checked his pupils—heck, he even checked his spine. The mother seemed annoyed with him, but he would not be rushed. Not this time.

"How was he before the rash started?"

She shrugged a little. "He said his skin hurt, but I didn't know exactly what that meant. I mean, it could be a paper cut, you know?"

"Did your throat hurt, buddy?" he asked the child, who nodded miserably, his blistered mouth puckering as he held back tears.

By the time he'd diagnosed him with Stevens-Johnson syndrome, likely triggered by the acetaminophen he'd been given after his annual shots, it was two o'clock. Daniel's stomach growled so loudly, people in the hallway were giving him weird looks. Winnie was at the nurses' station, as usual, her head bent in concentration over her work, her sunshine hair pulled back in a high ponytail. God, he loved her. He fingered the bracelet he'd bought her in his coat pocket. As if she sensed his attention, she looked up and smiled at him. "Did you eat already?"

He shook his head.

"Oh, good, me either. That's a happy coincidence. I'll just go get my food . . ."

"I'll go with you."

His exchange of words with Dr. Baker was still weighing on him, and now he had the joy of Winnie's presence without the pleasure of touching her. They'd agreed on no PDA at the hospital . . . but he wanted a taste of her. Just a tiny one.

"Everything okay?" Of course she would notice that he was stewing. Looking up and down the hall to see that the coast was clear, he pulled her into a supply closet and pressed her up against the door. Her lips met his, and comfort flowed through them. She gave a little hum of approval, and he felt his shoulders drop with relief. He hadn't been sure if this counted as PDA in her mind, since they weren't on display, even though they were at work, and he couldn't disappoint anyone else today. He pulled her closer, admittedly taking more than a little taste, and cradled her face in his hands.

Winnie pushed on his chest lightly, and he broke the kiss.

"You didn't answer my question."

CHAPTER
TWENTY-SIX

SHE DIDN'T WANT TO break the kiss, but he wasn't quite acting like himself. It was a distraction kiss, and she'd rather hear about the problem. Daniel sighed deeply, and his breath warmed her face. "It's complicated."

That troubled her, and she let her bag slide off her shoulder onto the floor to hold him better. "What happened?"

"I screwed up. A patient was having myocardial infarctions right in front of me, and I didn't see it."

"Oh, wow. That's not good."

He let out a rough laugh. "No. Not good."

"But someone must've caught it . . ."

"Martina." He shook his head, and she could see his frustration rising again. "I can't believe I didn't see it."

Winnie rubbed his arms, squeezing his shoulders to help relieve his tension. "You know, when my mom was a resident, she accidentally prescribed a medication that conflicted with what the patient was already taking. The man almost died. It happens to everyone sometime. I know you're doing your best, hon. Just be patient with yourself." She remembered the gift in her bag, and she bent to retrieve it. Winnie handed him the box with a coy smile. "Maybe this will cheer you up."

He quirked an eyebrow at her, and she just grinned. Cautiously, he opened the white box. "Oh, hey, it's Groot!"

"It's a plant." She smiled. "And don't worry, it claims it's very hard to kill, much like the actual Groot."

He smiled down at her, and she was immensely pleased with herself. "I got you something, too."

"You did? That's an odd coincidence."

"Like it was a coincidence last week when we got each other the same issue of *Spiderman*?"

"That was less of a coincidence, since we'd just talked about it over breakfast." He pulled out a bracelet with a tiny pink cupcake on it. "It's a charm bracelet," he explained needlessly. "I'll get you more parts to it as time goes by. But I liked this one, because you help people have a happy birthday and you have a thing for pink. And you're sweet."

He was staring down at her warmly, searching her face to see if she liked it, and Winnie felt a thought surge through her veins like a drug: *I want him.* Not because he wanted her, which was usually how it went with other men. A sort of mirrored desire; she liked being wanted, and the other person wanted her. But this wasn't that. This was 100 percent hers; her body demanded to own him, and it had very specific ideas about what it would do once it did. He was planning a future together, and she wanted that forever.

"Fred," he groaned, and he cursed under his breath. "You can't look at me like that."

"Like what?" She wanted to know what this deep desire looked like on her face.

"Like you want to burn all our clothes and see where it takes us."

"That'd be a good start," she said, playing with the top button of his coat, and his eyes narrowed.

"We promised . . ."

"Yes," she said softly. "And it's my fault. I'm sorry." She let her gaze fall to his neck, but he put his fingers under her chin to lift it back to his.

"I'm not. I want you to want me, I just . . . can't handle seeing it so plainly in your eyes right now. It's my problem, not yours." He lifted her arm and opened the clasp of the bracelet, putting it on her left wrist. A devilish thought came into her head, and she couldn't resist.

"Heroes are made by the path they choose, not the powers they are graced with."

Daniel's eyes fluttered closed. "So it's come to this. We're reduced to quoting Iron Man." He sighed, shaking his head. "Come on, let's go find somewhere a little more public to be right now, before I strip down and try your idea."

"I like Iron Man. He's ridiculous." She leaned closer to whisper in his ear. "But Thor's still my favorite . . ."

"Out, Fred. Exit the closet. Now." He pulled her gently away from the door to open it.

"Plus, even if we did burn our clothes, you know that's the moment Kyle would show up . . ."

Daniel cackled and gave her a big, smacking kiss on the cheek. "I love you, Fred."

"I love you, too."

She was still glowing when she got back to the nurses' station. Martina was eating carrot sticks that smelled lightly of vinegar, scrolling through an article about Prince Harry, ignoring an open textbook in front of her.

"A new batch of fermented carrot sticks? That extra brain power must be what's got you catching all those new doctors' mistakes."

Martina's tawny skin paled slightly. "Were they upset?"

"Daniel was upset with himself; he was very glad you caught it."

"I had to say something . . ."

"Of course you did! Don't be ridiculous."

"My auntie was the same way. No one caught hers, either, and she ended up with a lot of scarring. Heart attacks are so sneaky."

"Sounds like it." Winnie gave her a reassuring squeeze around the shoulders. "You did good." Her mother would object to her grammar, but it seemed to comfort Martina nonetheless. "How are your classes going?"

"Pretty good. It's kind of fun to be back in school. Plus, my dad always wanted to have a kid with a master's, now he'll have two."

Winnie grimaced. "Parental pressure is so fun."

"Oh, it's the best. But it actually is a good program. I'm enjoying it, for the most part; it's really interesting studying all the things that can happen in adult gerontology. And nurse practitioners get paid more, so hooray for money."

"We're quite the unlikely pair: I'm helping people into the world, as you help them out of it." She paused, not really ready to hear the answer to her next question. "And are you going to stay with us at Santiam once you're done?" Martina was part of what made being at the hospital fun, and Winnie wasn't interested in losing her in the nurses' station or as a friend.

Martina's eyes dropped to the keyboard. "I haven't decided yet."

"Well, I'd miss you."

Her friend bit a chunk off another carrot stick. "We'd still see each other. I promise."

"We'd better."

CHAPTER TWENTY-SEVEN

WINNIE WOKE TO THE sound of her phone ringing, blaring "Ride to Observatory" from the *Thor* movie soundtrack, a less than subtle nod to Daniel's status in her life.

"Hello?"

"Oh, thank God. Winifred, where are you?" Panic. Sandra Baker's voice was like a tidal wave, knocking Winnie awake. *Where are you?* Where *was* she? The living room was dark except for the TV, which had reverted to the Netflix menu. Someone's lovely, lean body was mostly under hers as she stretched. They must have fallen asleep watching TV again. Working strange hours, "Netflix and chill" was more like Netflix and pass out. Not that "chilling" was on the menu at the moment . . .

"Oh, I'm . . ." She made eye contact with her boyfriend's unfocused blue eyes just as she said, "I'm at Daniel's."

"Who is it?" he mouthed.

She mouthed back, "Mom."

"Good, bring him, too," Sandra went on. "He's good with women. Bring your bag."

Winnie sat up. "What's going on?"

"Penny Wallace's niece is visiting, and she's gone into early labor. She's hysterical, refusing to go to the hospital. We tried Nurse Mitton, but she's still in Dallas. The patient says she can't do this without her husband, who is on his way, but he's still in Boise."

"That's what, six, seven hours away?"

"At least."

Winnie searched for her shoes: not under the table, or under the couch . . .

"What time did her labor start?"

"Penny wasn't sure, Angela's been cagey about it. She only knew something was wrong because she wouldn't come out of the bathroom."

"We'll be right there." She hung up before she got the address. "Do you know where the Wallace place is?"

"Sure. We used to swim in their irrigation pond, which is pretty gross now that I think about it."

"Get your keys. Let's go." Winnie grabbed her bag from her car and filled him in on the way. Driving these back roads at night always made her nervous: deer were everywhere. People out here didn't seem to find them as cute as she did; not too surprising, considering they were tired of having their gardens eaten and their cars destroyed. She forced herself to calm down and prepare to be there for Angela, who must've been scared out of her mind.

They were walking up to the porch when the door flew open. Three women all started talking at her at once, one of them crying, and Winnie reached out to grab two of their hands. *Gee,* she thought, *I can't imagine why our laboring moth-*

er locked herself in the bathroom if this is the emotional climate of the room . . .

"Take a deep breath with me. Ready?" Winnie breathed in deeply through her nose and held it, looking into each of their eyes, until they'd all breathed in and held. Squeezing their hands, she slowly let it out and watched the tension drain from their shoulders. "One more." The look in her mother's eyes told her she was pushing it, but she ignored her. The two other women complied, and out of the corner of her eye, she noticed Daniel obeying as well. She hid her smile at that, but she let the happy feeling prompted by his support swim around inside her chest. "Okay. Now where's my patient?"

The nervous babble started up again, overlapping like a flock of birds fighting over a feeder. Winnie held up her hands, and they silenced again. "Who's Penny?"

A woman in her sixties with gray hair at her temples raised a timid hand.

"Okay, Penny, lead the way."

"She's locked the bathroom door," she reported over her shoulder as they started upstairs. "She won't open it for anyone, not even me. We've always been close, and I'm just so concerned—"

Winnie stopped her with a hand to the shoulder. "I'm here now. I've got it. I've worked with plenty of frightened mothers. It's late. You should all go to bed."

Penny's eyes widened. "Go to bed? While she's in labor?"

Winnie nodded. "It would be very helpful. A more peaceful atmosphere may convince her to come out, which would allow me to check her vitals and assess the baby's progress."

The older woman protested, and Winnie escorted her back downstairs as she listened to her concerns quietly.

"Those are some good points, and I'll keep them in mind," Winnie said over her shoulder as she started back up the stairs, Daniel trailing her.

It was the only closed door upstairs, between two bedrooms.

"Hi, Angela," Winnie said, resting her forehead against the door. "I'm Winifred. I'm a certified nurse midwife." She applauded herself inwardly for avoiding telling her she was Dr. Baker's daughter—the *d*-word would probably not put her at ease right now. "I just wanted to let you know that I'm here and I'm available if you want my help. I could hold your hand or get you a snack if you want. I've sent the others to bed, so it's just you and me."

Daniel cleared his throat.

"Oh," she corrected, "and Dr. Durand. Sorry, Dr. Durand."

"No doctors," Angela snapped, and Winnie winced. She'd forgotten her own advice so quickly. "I told them, I'm not giving birth yet." There was a pause. "Wait, did you say Durand? Which one?"

"The funny one," he called back, and Winnie rolled her eyes. "I think we met at the town picnic when you spent the summer with your Aunt Penny in '96."

"Oh, *Daniel* Durand?" Winnie heard the brass doorknob rattle as if Angela had put her hand to it, but it stayed firmly shut.

"If I unlock the door, you're going to make me go to the hospital, aren't you?"

"I won't make you do anything you don't want to do," Winnie replied gently. "In fact, I have a few ideas for how we might slow down labor until your husband arrives. Ironically, going to the hospital would probably be the stress you need to shut it down completely."

The door opened a crack to reveal a dark-haired woman with mascara running down her face. "Is that true?"

Winnie nodded, and the door opened wider, revealing Angela's whole face and belly.

"I usually tell my patients to delay as long as possible before they go. Something about fluorescent lights and the scent of disinfectant just doesn't put most women in the right headspace to—"

Angela gasped, pressing a hand to her lower back, her breaths becoming shallow. Winnie reached out to hold her other hand, waiting to continue until her body relaxed again.

"It sounds like you're doing slow breathing, is that right?"

Angela nodded lightly. "They said that was good for early labor."

"You're agitated enough that I'd like you to try variable breathing. So you'll start with a deep, cleansing breath at the start of the contraction, then we'll mix in more long breaths . . . Do you have a picture of your husband?"

"I do on my phone, but I think Aunt Penny has one of the whole family on her mantel."

"I'll get it," Daniel said, hopping to his feet. "You've gotta conserve your energy. Back in a flash."

The young mother beamed at him, but as soon as he was out of sight, Winnie saw her eyes fill with tears.

"This is our first baby," Angela sniffled, bracing her hands on the pink tile countertops. "I just wanted Ben to be here, I just wanted him to help me . . . I just wanted him to get to hold her right away."

"Of course you did. I imagine you're so disappointed." Winnie decided to take a chance, and she reached out to rest a hand on Angela's shoulder. "The good news is that your girl will be happy to meet him whenever he gets here, and I'm sure what he wants most is a safe, healthy birth for both of you. Do you think we can accomplish that here?"

"I don't know. I just can't go without him. I can't, I can't . . ."

"Okay. Let's think," Winnie said, nudging her way into the bathroom, hoping the patient wouldn't notice. It had Jack and Jill sinks, so they each leaned against one. "What if he pulled over and got a hotel room with good Wi-Fi? Instead of breaking the speed limits he's probably breaking right now?"

Angela gave her a watery smile. "Ben doesn't speed."

"Ben's never been a father before."

Angela smiled wider, then her eyebrows snapped together and her smile fell as another contraction came. The woman gripped both her hands as Winnie silently timed the contraction in her head. Almost a minute. That was a long one. But they were still at least five minutes apart; it was active labor, but it was early yet. First-time mothers often labored for hours, and her waters hadn't broken.

Daniel came back with the picture, a group shot from a wedding, Angela's from the look of it. She took it gratefully, smiling through tears at the faces of her family.

"Believe it or not, we're stoking the chemicals that are going to help you connect with your baby and help you get through labor right now."

"I believe it," she said, sliding down to the floor, her back against the wall. She sighed shakily. "Let's try to get him on the phone. I want to talk to him."

Winnie retreated to the hallway to give them a little privacy, and noticed that her mother, Penny, and her daughter Jennie were all crowded at the bottom of the stairs. She silently shooed them away, and the Wallaces glared at her disdainfully over their shoulders as they shuffled off in their robes and slippers. Her mother stayed, arms crossed, gaze thoughtful.

Half an hour later, Angela was settled in a warm bath with her husband on video chat, and she seemed much more relaxed. The heat must be helping her back labor. Winnie was lighting a lavender candle she'd brought as a quiet knock sounded at the door. *Must be Daniel.*

"Just a minute," she called softly. The tense look on her patient's face almost made her smile. How she'd gone from screaming through a locked door to not wanting Winnie out of her sight was a testament to her good training. "Be right back, Angela. I promise."

"Hi, Wonder Woman," he greeted, giving her a quick kiss as she closed the bathroom door most of the way behind her. "I'm going to take off. You don't need me here, and your mom can give you a ride home."

She frowned. Did he feel left out? He could be participating more, but Angela was still pretty leery of the doctors. She hoped she hadn't made him feel excluded. "Are you sure?"

He nodded. "I'm burning hours that I could be at the hospital; they need me more. You've got this under control."

"You got the door open. So thanks for coming."

"For you? Anything."

"Cheesy."

He kissed her again, longer this time, then grinned. "Good night, Fred. Text me when you get home, okay?"

"Good night, whippersnapper."

CHAPTER
TWENTY-EIGHT

EIGHT HOURS LATER, the situation was no longer calm.

"I want the hospital," cried Angela. "I want an epidural. I can't do this, I can't, I can't." Legs shaking, she clung to Winnie, whose back was about to give out.

"You're doing so great, babe," Ben called through the phone.

"Angela, I think you're going into transition. It wouldn't be safe for your girl to get into a car right now. I'd like to check your dilation again . . ." She'd been at six centimeters not long ago, and her water had broken all over Winnie as she was trying to check her. That had really catapulted Angela's body into action, which was a good thing. Once her water broke, they were on the clock to prevent infection. Winnie was now wearing a T-shirt one size too small that proclaimed she was part of the Timber Falls Track and Field 2004, and it was riding up in the back. She called it "the solidarity zone": Angela was basically naked in front of her aunt and cousin and Dr. Baker, and she was completely unashamed. And in light of that, Winnie wouldn't bring herself to care that her shorts were falling down and her shirt was riding up. Wardrobe problems were bound to happen during an unexpected birth: it was a law of nature.

"No," Angela moaned. "If I lie down, I won't be able to get up."

"The other two will hold you, and I'll check you standing." Winnie gestured to Penny and Jennie with her head, and they surged forward to support her, each under one arm. "You're doing great, Angela. So great."

"So great, babe!" her husband yelled through the phone, and she could tell he was close to crying. It must be tearing him up not to be there, but Angela hadn't wanted him driving in a compromised state on so little sleep.

Ten centimeters. Those last four centimeters had come fast. "Angela, if you feel like pushing on the next contraction, you can start—"

Angela let out a low, guttural yell as another contraction hit. That was the right kind of sound, and Winnie saw the top of the head appear. "I've got a visual on your baby!"

"Really?" Angela whimpered, shuddering. "I'm almost done?"

"Do you want to see, Ben?" Winnie called.

There was a pause, and the room stilled momentarily to hear his answer. "No, I'm good." All four women laughed, wiping tears and sweat; the bathroom had a heat lamp that wasn't doing them any favors in the enclosed space.

"I love you, Ben," Angela called, and he echoed it back to her. Winnie put a hand on her patient's belly and could feel the muscles tightening.

"Here comes another one . . ."

"Oh my—" Angela cried, then her words dissolved into a yell, and a little more of the head appeared. As the contraction ebbed, Winnie grabbed a towel to make sure she didn't drop the slippery little person. But it proved premature: over the next few minutes, Angela's labor stalled. Her contractions were still strong, but she just wasn't pushing as hard as she needed to. Winnie tried not to be frustrated, but she was tired, too. She wanted this over—without an ambulance ride or emergency C-section.

"How are you doing, helpers?" Winnie asked the relatives. "Does anyone need to tap out?"

Penny shook her head, but Jennie's lip trembled.

"If she can do it, I can do it," she said, her voice breaking. "You're my hero, Ang!"

Fire. That's what was in Angela's eyes. "Can I push now? Between contractions?"

"If you want to. If you can. It'll be more productive if you wait, but it's your birth. You're in control here."

Angela's chest was heaving. "I want to get on my knees." With shaking arms, they lowered her to the ground and painstakingly turned her to face the edge of the tub. She leaned over, resting her head on her arms, and Winnie quietly moved to be behind her. When the next contraction hit, she was ready. Angela pushed hard, and Winnie shoved her fingers up to check that the cord wasn't around the baby's neck. "You're almost done, Angela. Once we get past her shoulders, it's easy. You're gonna hold your baby in just a minute. Then you'll just deliver the placenta, and you'll be done."

"I can do this, I can do this," Angela whimpered into her arms. "Ben?"

"I'm here, honey," he choked out. "So to speak."

Angela chuckled, and another contraction hit. The head crowned, and Winnie supported the baby, even as she cheered

Angela on. Two more contractions and she slid out. Angela collapsed, crying, and Winnie put her baby immediately on her chest. Best as she could, she cleaned up the baby with the damp corner of a beach towel from Fort Lauderdale. Life really was a strange thing, and she never felt that more strongly than during a birth. Time seemed to slow. Jennie cut the cord; placenta came and went. She didn't ask if they wanted to keep it; they didn't seem the type. The women helped Angela into the empty tub and settled her daughter in her arms. Winnie thought Penny and Jennie might leave, but they just sat down together on the closed toilet seat, holding hands, staring at Angela and the baby with tears in their eyes.

"That was so beautiful," Jennie whispered as Angela cooed to her baby. "I can't believe you get to do that all the time."

"Best job in the world," Winnie said with a smile. "You were a great help. Couldn't have done it without you." She turned to Angela. "It's time to let your girl eat." The relatives did leave then, and Winnie brought the phone over to give Ben a better look. His snuffling sobs almost outdid his daughter's noises as she rooted for the breast, and Angela laughed through her tears.

"Can I get back in the car now?" he asked meekly.

Angela nodded. "You better be here when I wake up."

"I will be. I promise. I want to kiss you and hold you and tell you you're amazing. I want to hold Charlotte."

"That's a beautiful name," Winnie told them softly.

"You haven't heard the whole thing yet," Angela said, still watching her baby nurse. "Charlotte Winifred Jones." She glanced up at Ben. "Is that okay?"

"Totally okay," he replied, wiping his face. "Absolutely."

Winnie was speechless; she smiled at her patient and handed her the phone. She needed a moment to compose herself: she felt the strain of having so many people leaning on her to know what to do. Leaving the door open, Winnie stepped out into the hallway and felt cooler immediately. Penny was hauling a large metal apparatus up the stairs.

"We use this to weigh the lambs. I thought it might be useful."

Winnie laughed. "Yes, thanks. I'll sanitize it, then we can weigh Charlotte." She sucked in a breath as Penny's face contorted. "Oh, please don't tell Angela I ruined the surprise of her name. I'm just so tired, and it just slipped out, and—"

Penny put down the scale and pulled Winnie into a hug. "The secret's safe with me."

As Penny stepped away, Winnie noticed her mother sitting on the bottom step, her head tilted to rest against the wall. In an exhausted haze, Winnie went and sat down next to her mom.

"You can go home, if you want," said Winnie. "I know you're tired. Penny's husband can give me a ride a little later."

"I was wrong."

"About what?" Without turning to her, Winnie took her mom's hand and squeezed. She wasn't sure where this conversation was going, and her brain was fuzzy enough to doubt that she had the self-control to keep it civil. It sounded good, sounded like the right direction, but . . . she'd thought that before. Her trust felt fragile.

"I've been seeing someone. Nick Sokolov, he's a dermatologist. And I was trying to tell him about you and your work, when I realized I didn't really know anything about you and

your work." She huffed a laugh. "We work in the same building, lived in the same house. I should've known more."

You assumed a lot, Winnie wanted to say. *You assumed you
didn't need to know, because you assumed it was temporary.*

"But watching you with this patient, I see what a good rap-
port you were able to build. Your technique is different, and
I see why this might be a good solution for people who have
trust issues with doctors."

"Thank you." Winnie knew that her mother would never
be able to admit that it was a good option for many other types
of patients as well, so she counted it as a small victory and said
nothing. A scent floated to her from deeper into the house. *Bacon.* Someone was cooking bacon, and Winnie's stomach made
a noise akin to an angry walrus. She patted her mother's hand
and rose, but Sandra caught her arm. "And I was wrong about
Daniel. He does care about you. I told him he could go home,
but he wanted to make sure you were okay." She swallowed. "I
shouldn't have meddled in your relationships. I apologize."

"You're forgiven, Mom," Winnie said, giving her mother a
tight hug that lasted far longer than usual. "Well, you're forgiv-
en for that. Not for keeping your boyfriend a secret. That we're
going to have to discuss in greater detail first."

Sandra laughed softly, blushing, and Winnie felt her face
break into a huge smile. "You like this guy."

"I do. He's great."

"You told me he was boring and bad at conversation!"

"I lied." She shrugged. "I was scared. I haven't felt this way
about anyone since . . ."

"Since Dad?"

Sandra nodded, and Winnie clapped her hands quietly. "I can't wait to meet him."

"Good. Now I smell cinnamon rolls."

"It's bacon."

Sandra gave her a mischievous look. "Let's settle this once and for all." Dragging her forward, she called, "Mr. Wallace, what's for breakfast?"

CHAPTER
TWENTY-NINE

DÉJÀ VU. Winnie felt time was repeating itself as she sipped a glass of Riesling, leaning on the marble bar at her grandparents' house, standing next to Daniel. Except this time, instead of looking over a ballroom full of acquaintances and strangers, she was looking at a living room full of her family and friends, getting to know each other. Her grandfather was talking animatedly with Daniel's dad about politics; Farrah was standing with her grandmother, admiring souvenirs from her world travels. Daniel's brother Philip rubbed his wife Claire's shoulders as teenage Maggie, Daniel's sister, played with Cooper. Her mother had brought her new boyfriend, Nicolai, and they were chatting with Kyle.

"Doesn't she have the most beautiful skin?" Dr. Sokolov trailed the back of his knuckles down her mother's cheek, and Winnie suppressed a grin as her fair-skinned mother went red as a stop sign. Yet there was nothing in her body language that said "stop." Kyle uncomfortably muttered something Winnie couldn't hear, and she winked at him when he caught her eye. Now Dr. Sokolov was offering her mother a bruschetta appetizer, and she was actually eating it . . .

"Forget about *us* going eight weeks celibate," Daniel whispered. "Your mom's not going to make it eight weeks. Your mom's not going to make it one week."

"Stop talking about my mom's sex life," Winnie hissed. "And my mother doesn't believe in sex before marriage."

"She might be rethinking that position," he said, then snickered. "Position."

"Oh, grow up, Daniel."

He nudged her. "Whatever. You laughed. I heard you."

"I did no such thing." She twirled her glass on the bar. "We should go rescue your brother from the lovebirds."

"Nah. He deserves the punishment for all the times he's interrupted us."

"That's savage, bae."

Daniel laughed so hard, Winnie thought he was going to give himself a strangulated hernia; the family paused their conversations to turn to and grin at them. He looped his arm around her shoulders and pulled her into his side, pressing a kiss to her temple. "God, I love you so much. Thank you for overcoming the language barrier between us, Fred."

"I love you, too. And thank you for overcoming the parental barrier between us."

"Can I have your attention, please?" Her grandfather raised his voice above the others. "I just want to thank you all for allowing us to host Easter. It's a privilege and a pleasure to have so many wonderful people in our home. The prime rib will be done in a few minutes, so grab another cocktail, and we'll make our way into the dining room in a few minutes." He cleared his throat. "And if I may say so, I hope this is a shade of things to come."

Winnie felt emotion clog her own throat as well. She didn't have a father whose blessing Daniel could ask, but her grandfather had just made his feelings clear on the matter. She lifted her glass in salute, fighting back tears, and he lifted his in response.

MARTINA WAS STARING. Sitting next to Winnie at the nurses' station, she was taking big, juicy bites of her Pink Lady apple and just . . . watching her.

"Can I help you?" Winnie asked, not looking up from the computer screen.

"Today's eight weeks; the bet's over. You won."

"How do you know that?"

Martina rolled her eyes. "I did *math*. So?"

"So . . . what?" Yes, she was committed to not talking about this. Staunchly.

Her friend leaned closer, pitching the apple core into the wastebasket. "So, are you going to . . . ?"

Winnie bit her lip. "I don't know."

"You *don't know*?" Martina hissed. "If I were you, I wouldn't even be at work today. I'd have called in sick and spent all day—"

"Yes, yes, all right, well, I'm not you, Nurse Lopez. We've just been busy, okay? We have a hard enough time connecting without trying to find a time for . . ."

"Connecting," Martina said, lowering her voice to an alto register, as her eyebrows bounced.

"Stop it," Winnie whispered sharply. "We are at *work*."

"Well, in this department particularly, I'm pretty sure people know how it works."

Winnie giggled, then made herself stop. "No. I'm not talking about this now. I'm sure Daniel and I will find time to celebrate . . . eventually. There's no rush." Her body vehemently disagreed with that statement, but she was saving a lot of money on her electricity bill due to all the cold showers she was taking. That was . . . a plus. But the truth was that she was disappointed. She hadn't expected rose petals strewn over her bed or a seven-course dinner, but she'd expected *something*; some acknowledgment that the bet was over and they'd prevailed over the forces of lust and motherly concern. She picked up her Thor bobblehead and scowled at him for a long moment before putting him back down on the desk with a thud. *Really, Daniel?* And more than that, it was 2:01. He hadn't even come by to flirt with her.

She went back to her paperwork with resignation in her heart. She'd known what they were getting into with two difficult schedules. She'd just be . . . flexible, that's all. Understanding. Forgiving. *Not a big deal, not a big deal, not—*

A low, out-of-breath voice interrupted her pep talk to herself. "Nurse Baker, can you come out from behind the nurses' station, please?" Her annoyance got the better of her, and she decided that if he was going to be too busy for her, two could play that game.

"Sorry, I'm really behind, I just need a few more minutes to—" She looked up to find him nowhere. "Daniel?"

"Down here."

She peeked over the Formica counter, expecting to find him tying a shoe or greeting a small patient. She did not expect to see him on one knee, holding up a white gold engagement ring with a square emerald winking up at her, his baby-blue scrub shirt covered in vomit. *Now? At work? Like this?*

"What is happening right now?" she whispered.

"Sorry I'm late," he whispered back. "Kid threw up on me." He whipped the shirt off and tossed it away as if it were an inconvenience, simply something unwanted that had stuck to him.

"Babe, you could've changed . . ." But thank God he hadn't; she'd been aching to get a look at that chest for weeks now, but she hadn't dared. But now . . . *Worth. The. Wait.* Winnie wanted to pinch herself to make sure this was really happening.

"No. This is more important. And it's already 2:10, so I'm fifteen minutes late as it is. Your friendly neighborhood fiancé shouldn't do that to you . . . and I needed to say this before anything else happened today."

All her annoyance vanished. Winnie felt her face break into such a huge smile, she was surprised it fit on her face.

Daniel took a deep breath and held up the ring a little higher. "Winifred Baker, when you nervously looked into my eyes and told me about the bet you'd made with your mother, you put a lot of faith in me. You believed that everything I'd told you was true and not a lame attempt to get you into bed."

"Little ears," she said, still nervous apparently, tipping her head meaningfully toward Annabelle Gardner, who was staring at them, wide-eyed.

"Right. Sorry," he chuckled, then cleared his throat and sobered. "When you told me with such sincerity that this could be something good, I knew in my heart that it already was. And with any luck, it still will be eighty years from now."

Laughter bubbled up out of her, uncontainable. "Only eighty?"

"Even with my excellent skin care regimen, I don't think either of us wants to see what I'll look like past one hundred."

"You're so vain," she giggled, then suddenly noticed the crowd that had formed around the half-naked doctor, and her gaze fell back on Daniel, still on the ground, still holding up the ring. A blonde head at the edge of the group caught her eye: her mother stood watching them, obvious tears in her eyes, one hand covering her mouth. Dr. Baker gave her a small nod, and Winnie smiled. She didn't crave her mother's acceptance anymore, but it was nice to have it nonetheless.

"Um, Win? Are you going to answer?"

"You didn't ask me anything," she replied primly, and the crowd bubbled with soft laughter.

"Always making me work for it," he grumbled, still grinning. "Winifred Elizabeth Baker, will you please let me be your sidekick till death do us part? Will you marry me?"

"Of course I will."

He was up off the floor and kissing her over the counter before she could even get a proper look at the ring. After a moment, Daniel vaulted himself over the counter and brought her into his arms as the crowd chattered and giggled excitedly.

"Kyle's going to be out tonight," he whispered in her ear, lips grazing her lobe, and she was amazed no one ran for the fire extinguisher given how her body had assuredly just burst into flames. Being held by a shirtless Daniel was definitely a fire hazard.

"Okay, but if he interrupts this time . . ."

"He won't. I promise. Not brothers, not mothers, no one. And if they try, I'll kill them myself." He kissed her again, longer and deeper than was really appropriate with so many people watching, but Winnie couldn't bring herself to care. She wanted this man, however she could get him, whatever he was willing to give her. Daniel caressed her face tenderly. "Nothing's going to keep us apart anymore, Fred. I promise."

Something good indeed.

EPILOGUE

TWO YEARS LATER

"Breathe, honey." Daniel rubbed Winnie's neck, trying to ease her tension, even as he watched her fetal monitor begin to spike with another contraction. Her back rose and fell rapidly under the thin cotton of the long nightgown she'd chosen to labor in. Fourteen hours in, he'd hoped that things would be going better than this.

"I *am* breathing, Daniel," Winnie snapped. "If I wasn't breathing, I'd be dead." She was on her hands and knees on the hospital bed, her blonde hair curtaining her face, and she began to rock forward and back, moaning as another contraction hit.

"Breathe slower, I mean." The monitor was really distracting, and he didn't notice how patronizing his tone was. She was, after all, a far greater expert on childbirth than he was.

"Do you want to be here to meet your daughter or not?"

"You're not gonna kick me out." He grinned, getting down on his knees on the cold gray tile to face her. "You love me. You married me. I'm a keeper."

"You are," she muttered, pressing her damp forehead against his dry one. "You are a keeper. Now go turn off that stupid music, will you?" He had to agree; for such mellow instrumental music, it did not seem to be calming her down. He

225

nudged the exercise ball she'd tried bouncing on out of his way, but tripped over the aromatherapy heating pack she'd rejected. When he came back to her, Winnie looked utterly dejected.

"Harder than you thought?" he whispered, and she nodded, closing her eyes.

"I'm just so tired. I didn't know this kind of tiredness was even possible." Her shaking arms buckled, and she went to her elbows, groaning. "Maybe I should've taken the drugs." Her admission shocked him and impressed him at the same time; it took a lot of humility to admit you might have been wrong, that what was right for someone else might not be right for you.

"But you're doing amazing. So amazing. And you're getting closer . . ." He rose to go check on her progress, but she reached out and grabbed at his clothes.

"No, no. Stay here," she panted. "Right now, you're my partner and her daddy, not the doctor."

"I think I can be both," he said, craning his neck, but she yanked him back to the front of the bed by his T-shirt, and he chuckled, rubbing his tired eyes under his glasses. "Fine, you're in charge."

"That's right," she said, and despite being a sweaty, laboring mess, she somehow still managed to retain that primness that had so attracted him to her. Despite that tender thought, he couldn't keep the concern off his face, and she saw it.

"I'm running out of time, aren't I?" she asked softly. Another contraction hit, and he got up to press inward on her hips as she groaned loudly. His muscles shook; his arms were starting to get as tired as the rest of him . . . He hadn't gotten much sleep in the last forty-eight hours, and it was messing with his head. He returned to the front of the bed to see her eye-to-eye.

"This is not your fault, Fred," he said sternly. "These things happen; she's pressing on the cord. Babies do that. That's why I insisted on the hospital, babe. Your health and our daughter's health are the most important things. How many times have you told mothers that? Embrace it, lady. You're gonna have a C-section."

He saw the tears shining in her eyes, but she nodded, letting her forehead rest on her arms. "I can't believe this. I'm sorry. I'm sorry I failed you."

"What?" He scowled, feeling his anger rise like floodwaters. "Winifred, that is *not true*. Not at all."

"I know, but . . ." Hearing the wobble in her voice felt like someone had punched him in the gut.

"But nothing!" His voice rang off the pink walls; he shouldn't be yelling at a laboring mother. He was probably stressing her out. But the fatigue and the tension meant the yelling kept coming. "You *know* that's not true, I've had to listen to you rant about this time and time again. If the roles were reversed, you'd slap me for saying that!"

"You're right." She sniffled. "I would. It just feels different on this side of it; my brain's all messed up." His heart went out to her; none of this was simple. None of it.

"Well, you'll never hear the word 'failure' from my lips where our daughter's birth is concerned."

She nodded. "Is my mom freaking out?"

"No, she knows you're in good hands." It was a bald-faced lie; he'd put his phone on 'do not disturb' an hour ago because he was tired of her panicky text messages. Dr. Baker had been confined to the waiting room per Winnie's request.

"Okay. But you'll be in the operating room with me?" Her voice was small, and when she lifted her head again, Winnie's eyes glimmered with fatigue and fear. It was almost comical; his experienced, confident wife was asking questions she absolutely knew the answer to, suddenly needy and wanting reassurance, doubting things she'd known for years. He felt like he was back at Kyle's house when she'd shown up unexpectedly after dropping the truth bomb on her mom, holding her as they lay on the couch, trying to show her how much he cared. His guess was that while she felt in control here, laboring, her confidence was crumbling at the thought of needing interventions. Daniel was having a hard time not being knocked off his feet by this as well; he wanted to take charge, but he knew he couldn't. The operating room wasn't a comfortable space for either of them, and they were both all too aware of the risks involved with surgery.

"Nothing could keep me away," he assured her, rubbing her arm in what he hoped was a soothing way. It was harder than he thought, too. His mind pitched forward to what was next: he'd need to scrub and change. It was probably overkill, but this was his kid and his wife they were talking about. God forbid he make them sick in some way—

"Daniel," Winnie said.

"Hmm?"

"Go tell them."

"Oh, right."

"And Daniel," she said, pulling him back, putting them nose to nose. They paused in that awkward position as another strong contraction hit, and Winnie's face contorted with pain before it cleared once more. "No unnecessary watchers. I have to be able to look these people in the eye later."

"Got it. No interns." He kissed her forehead, and he could smell the lavender she'd used. Daniel started out of the room, but saw the tiny bottle of lavender oil sitting by the door, and on impulse, he quickly slathered some on his neck. He needed all the calm right now. All these intense decisions, all this stress was taking a toll on him, and the helplessness had him feeling desperate.

Frances Mitton looked up as he approached the nurses' station. "She agreed?"

"Well, she doesn't really have a choice, but yes, she did."

The older woman smiled, rising from her office chair. "She'll be in very good hands, I promise."

"Come on, I'll help you change." Daniel blinked; Kyle had taken him by the elbow and was leading him down the hall toward the OR. He looked over his shoulder; he hadn't even noticed his parents, his siblings, his mother-in-law, and Winnie's grandparents sitting in the waiting room. He waved at them, and they waved back.

"You look freaked out."

"I *am* freaked out."

"Everything will probably be fine. This hospital has an excellent record regarding C-sections." Leave it to his level-headed brother to calm him down with his constant rationality.

Smiling, Daniel toed off his shoes as Kyle pulled out the teal scrubs. "How would you know?"

"I looked it up."

Daniel stood still, his hands in mid-pull of his shirt, just staring at him.

"What?" Kyle asked, perplexed. "She's my sister-in-law, I was concerned."

"That's sweet, bro."

"Whatever. Take off your shirt." He'd rolled the scrub shirt up toward the collar, like he would have done for a child, and was waiting for him to lift his arms. Daniel was too tired to complain. It gave him a burst of energy, being cared for instead of tripping over himself, trying to anticipate Winnie's every need. Eyes closed, he took a moment to remind himself that he wasn't alone. The family was here. They couldn't affect the outcome any more than he could, but they were *here*.

Once he'd gotten changed and moved their stuff to the recovery room, he was back by her side. The placement of the spinal had not gone well, and he could feel the tension between her and the medical staff. She wouldn't let go of his hand as they put her hair up, and he stretched to pull up a chair next to her head. He knew nothing he could say would be enough, so he just gazed into her eyes, trying to reassure her without words, brushing his fingers over her pale cheek; the operating room was freezing. As they put up the pale-blue barrier, Daniel felt they'd created a little room just for them. There were so many things he wanted to tell her, but he held back, knowing it was nothing he hadn't told her before: *You're my hero. I'm so glad you're mine. You inspire me. I love you so much.* He felt hot, unbidden tears come to his eyes. *I don't know what I'd do without you. Nothing can happen to you. I need you.*

"Uh-oh," Winnie said, squeezing his hand even tighter. "Shit just got real, huh?"

"Man, you used to be so proper," he laughed, wiping his tears. "Who taught you to talk like that?"

"You did, whippersnapper," she whispered, putting a hand to his cheek. "It's gonna be okay, honey. We'll both be okay."

"I know."

During the surgery, Daniel couldn't keep still. His leg bounced incessantly, and he kept rolling his shoulders, as if that would help the tension that had clamped down on them like a vise. He jumped every time an instrument dropped onto the metal tray. He knew these doctors and nurses, but the urge to stand up and see what was happening was overwhelmingly strong. The only thing keeping his backside cemented to the hard chair was Winnie. She was hanging on to him for dear life.

"What's going on over there? Are they almost done?" Her voice seemed muted and echoey through the oxygen mask.

"How should I know? I'm just the daddy. The doctors are over there."

"Almost done," Dr. Waters assured them. "Just another minute."

"We're gonna meet our baby soon," she whispered, and she managed a grin that made him relax a tiny bit. And then a baby's cries broke his focus, and he jumped up from his chair.

"Well, Dad?" the surgeon asked, as he lifted out the squealing, flailing person with a smile. "You want to cut the cord?" Daniel hesitated for just a moment, then hurried over, trying not to look at his wife's far-too-open body. With a snip, they whisked her away briefly to get cleaned up and weighed. Then she was back, and the nurse was putting his daughter into his arms. Which nurse? Who cared. His girl was finally here, with a head full of wispy blonde hair and what was clearly his mother's nose. She'd be horrified, he thought with glee. Daniel whipped off his shirt and took his daughter into his arms, cradling her against his skin. He'd been so jealous of Winnie during their whole pregnancy: getting to feel her fluttery kicks, her rolls, and yes, even her bladder punches. He was dying to know this little person.

"Hey. Hey, Kendall. I'm your dad." At the sound of his words, the baby calmed, snuggling into his chest, and his heart went supernova with joy. "She knows my voice!" He sat back in the chair, relishing the feeling . . . but it was ruined by the cold. And if he was cold, Kendall probably was, too. He pulled his shirt over her protectively, but paused when he noticed a mark on her back.

"What's that? Winnie, what is that?"

She squinted from the operating table. "Looks like a birthmark."

"Oh, right." *Of course it was.* Had he forgotten even the most basic medical knowledge since becoming a father? He was relieved no one else had heard him. "What a beautiful girl you are," he cooed to her, "and someday, you can grow up and be whatever kind of doctor you want to be."

"Daniel . . ." Winnie's tone held a warning, which he ignored.

"There are so many specialities to choose from," he went on. "Your grandpa and I are both family doctors, like your great-grandpa was. But don't let that sway you. Uncle Kyle's in the emergency room. Your uncle Philip is a physical therapist. Those are good options, too."

Then Daniel felt something warm and wet running down his abs, and he laughed. "Seriously, kid? I thought we were having a moment!"

Winnie laughed, too. "You *were* having a moment. Moments are messy sometimes. But I guess we know how she feels about having her career dictated."

"She clearly has your backbone." He grinned, rubbing Kendall's back gently.

"And your determination," Winnie added. He blushed at that; Winnie was still in awe of how he dealt with his dyslexia. Much more than he thought he deserved.

"She's got my mom's nose, don't you think?" He'd never felt more like a giant, just comparing the size of his hand to her whole body. He was definitely going to need a newborn photo shoot to document this incredible child. He used to think all babies looked the same, but this baby was clearly his, and his heart sang just to look at her.

"I don't know," Winnie said, cocking her head. "I see a lot of you in her, too. I bet she has your eyes."

"I hope she's got yours." He shifted to look into his baby's eyes, trying to see her better, even knowing that she couldn't focus on his face yet. Then a thought made him sober. "What if she's dyslexic?"

"Then you'll be able to teach her all about it," she said, yawning. "It didn't stop your dreams. It won't stop hers, either. She's got a huge cheering squad who'll help her every step of the way. And speaking of help," Winnie said softly, reaching out to put a hand on his leg, "she's probably ready to try nursing."

"In a minute," he said, still staring at Kendall as she gave a yawn that seemed impossibly large for such a small person.

"We're tired, Mama. It's been a big day." He glanced at Winnie, grinning. "That's your mom, Kendall. She's excited to meet you, too, she's just busy right now. She's really great. You're gonna love her. I sure do."

"And I love you," Winnie replied, crooking a finger for him to come closer. And as he gently pressed his lips to hers, surrounded by his two favorite people, Daniel could feel nothing but complete contentment . . . damp pants and all.

Would you write a review?

Daniel and Winnie, they make quite a pair.
If you agree, do you think you could share
on Goodreads or Amazon, wherever you lurk?
I'll tell you a secret: it so helps my work.
And getting to hear that you loved them, too?
Well, it makes my whole week. Believe me. It's true.

There's a reason why I'm a novelist and not a poet, but in all seriousness, I would be so appreciative if you could spread the word about this series! It's a huge help to my business. Thanks!

Don't miss a moment of Timber Falls fun!

Could Be Something Good (Daniel and Winnie)
Must be a Mistake (Kyle and Ainsley—keep reading for a sneak peek!)
Right Back Where We Started (Martina and Crash)

Coming Winter 2020...

More Than We Bargained For (Starla and Sawyer)
Never Say Never (Lizzie and Chase)
Maybe It's Just Me (Maggie and R.J.)

Also by Fiona West

The Borderline Chronicles (sweet fantasy romance)
The Ex-Princess: a chronically-ill princess who fled from her responsibilities is forced to face the fiancé she abandoned and journey across a magically-unpredictable continent. Can she keep the life she's given up everything to build?
The Un-Queen: a king caught between love and legality...can Abbie and Edward's relationship survive engagement and the opposition who wants to tear them apart again?
The Jinxed Journalist: a single mother gets her dream job as a journalist, only to find herself caught in royal scandal, opposing her son's new mentor. When forced to choose between love and her career, can she still come out a winner?
The Semi-Royal: a doctor takes an expedition with her brother's best friend that has life-changing results. Can she resist the underlying attraction that's been there for years?
The Almost-Widow: a security professional finds herself paired with a shy, sensory-sensitive man on the night watch. Can their friendship blossom into something more?

Must Be a Mistake, coming June 19th, 2020!

Read on for a sneak peek at Chapters One and Two!

————— ⟨∾⟩ —————

CHAPTER ONE

AINSLEY SIGHED AS HER first graders lined up for library; Cooper Durand was still in the Naughty Chair. She didn't refer to it that way in front of her students, of course . . . she called it the Think It Over Chair. A place for them to take a deep breath, regain their self-control in a safe area . . . but that didn't changes its stripes: it was a Naughty Chair. And Cooper certainly belonged there: she'd caught him peeing on a tree at recess instead of getting the pass to go inside. She'd happened to see him out her window today as she was eating lunch alone in her room, and she nearly choked on her chicken salad sandwich. She'd asked Mrs. Talbot, the classified lady who had recess duty to watch out for him, but recess was a pretty hectic place as it was, and Mrs. Talbot's eyesight wasn't what it used to be. This was only the instance she knew about, but there could be more. A *lot* more. They got a morning and afternoon recess . . . she sighed again. Ainsley reached out a hand toward him.

"Cooper, come lead the line with me, please." The boy bounded up and trotted over to the head of the line. She held his hand as the class meandered down the hall, looking less like a line and more like a dodecahedron. "What did you do that you shouldn't have done?"

"Pee on the tree when you were looking."

"So close," she said, schooling her face into a stern but kind look. "Try again."

"Pee on the tree."

"Better. And what did you *not* do that you *should've* done?"

"Get the pass from Mrs. Talbot." He looked up at her, genuinely frustrated. "But Kacie and Fran always get it first and they take too long! Recess is over by the time they come back."

"Well, they're not supposed to go together anyway, so I'll talk to Mrs. Talbot, okay?" She squeezed his hand, and he gave her a semi-toothless grin.

"Thanks, Miss Buchanan." He paused. "Don't worry, I peed on a different one every day, so one wouldn't grow taller. Uncle Kyle says urine is a good fertilizer."

"Yes, well . . . that's a relief. Also, maybe don't listen to everything Uncle Kyle says."

"Why not?" He whispered, because they'd reached the closed library doors.

"Because little boys don't need to know the agricultural applications for urine," she whispered back, turning to smile at the librarian, C.J. "See you later, Buchanan's Bunch." She had sixty-two ten squares calling her that weren't going to cut out and laminate themselves. She'd have a talk with Uncle Kyle later . . . if she could get him to talk to her at all. *Whatever.* Lots of other fish in the sea. Less grunty, broody fish. Well, *some* other fish in the sea. More like a lake, really. And at that moment, it was feeling downright puddle-ish. She'd been on four dates with Todd Glazer...all of which were boring. When he called for a fifth, she let him down gently.

Ainsley blitzed through the afternoon math lesson and ended up with time to spare—everything this time of year was just a review of kindergarten—so they read Lily's Big Day by Kevin Henkes again. Her students never got tired of hearing a story about a child (well, a mouse child) who wanted desperately to be her teacher's flower girl, who wanted to be special to the people she loved. It was so delightfully relatable to them.

Posey raised her hand. "Are you going to get married, Ms. Buchanan?"

"Yes, I think so. Someday." She smiled at the kids, who were beaming at her. "Do you think I'd pick one of you to be my flower person?"

"No," the kids chorused, giggling. *Oh good; they actually listened to the story.* When she walked her gaggle of skipping, yawning, babbling students out to the buses, Kyle Durand was there to pick up Cooper, who broke ranks to run to him. Kyle Freaking Durand, with his tousled brown hair, so dark it was almost black. His stormy brown eyes, the physique that showcased the benefits of daily exercise. He greeted his nephew too quietly to be heard over the melee of students. The boy nodded, then shook his head, apparently reconsidering his first answer to whatever question he'd asked. Kyle looked up and caught her gaze. "He had a rough day?"

There was a momentary stand-off: he stared at her, as if he was waiting for her to come to him or shout her answer across the hoards still pairing student with caregiver or mode of transportation. She crossed her arms and stared right back. With half a grin, he sauntered over to her slowly as if she didn't have another ten kids waiting for her to put them on the bus. *What the heck is so funny?*

"In the future, I'd appreciate it if you encouraged Cooper to keep his tree-watering activities confined to your own yard."

His eyes snapped to the boy in horror. "You *didn't*."

"I had a good reason!" Cooper shouted.

Dr. Durand ran a hand down his face. "It won't happen again; sorry."

"Well, I'm satisfied with the time he's served in the Think It Over Chair, but I wanted to make someone at home aware of the . . . issue."

"Sure, yes. I will pass the message on to Philip. Sorry about that; I just figured it's the kind of thing the boy should know, in case of a zombie apocalypse."

Ainsley smiled in spite of herself. "A what?"

"Zombie apocalypse," Kyle said, his brown eyes somber despite his ridiculous statement. How he kept a straight face, she'd never know. "We've gotta prepare the kids for what's coming. As an educator, you play a key role, I'm surprised you don't know all about it."

"Thank you for your time, Dr. Durand," Ainsley said, still smiling, walking backward, leading the line toward the rest of the buses. "See you Monday."

"Only if the zombies don't attack first," he called back, and several teachers around them stopped to stare. Ainsley didn't let herself laugh until she turned to put Damon, Denver and Heaven on Bus #6.

CHAPTER TWO

KYLE SLAMMED HIS TRUCK door. What had gotten into him? Her shirt, that's what. She was wearing that blouse he liked, the dark blue see-thru one with the rainbow trout on it. How she managed to make rainbow trout look cute and hot at the same time, he hadn't been able to figure out. And he had spent considerable time thinking about it. . . while doing his laundry, at family dinners, working at the hospital. . . he felt a bit bad about that last one. But when he wasn't working, he didn't feel bad thinking about Ainsley. He was a good multi-tasker. He'd been doing it for years anyway. If he hadn't gone to that dumb wedding, he wouldn't have this problem.

"Are we going home or what?" Cooper called from the back seat. Kyle slid on his sunglasses and muttered under his breath about brothers and their unreasonable expectations. He'd agreed to pick up his nephew right after Philip had his second baby, and now, it was somehow expected he'd do it every day. If he didn't get to see Ainsley, he'd have pawned Coop off on his mom weeks ago.

"Of course we are."

"Then why are we just sitting here? I'm hungry."

"You're always hungry. It's amazing your dad has any money at all..."

"I'm a growing boy. That's what Mom says." That did sound like Claire. Besides, the kid wasn't overweight. No one could figure out where he put it all; his belly was like a black hole.

Kyle started the truck and turned out onto the main road. The buses had already left. Ainsley had gone back inside. He'd realized something, engaged in a silent battle of wills over something as simple as a short conference. She was never going to come to him. Though he'd never said it out loud, that's what he'd been waiting for, all this time. Waiting for her to see him, waiting for her to figure out why he tagged along with his brother as often as possible. But it wasn't going to happen. . . so what were his other options? During that short walk across the concrete pick up area, he'd weighed them: 1. Give up. If his infatuation with her had lasted this long, he didn't think it would probably die just because he wanted it to, just because he was scared. It was like a raccoon in a koi pond; it just kept coming back. He suspected that his autism was playing a role in his fascination with her, but he couldn't be sure. 2. Keep waiting. That hadn't worked so far. 3. Go after her. It wasn't like he hadn't thought of it. He had, of course he had. But it wasn't his style; he'd never needed to before. In high school and in college, he'd had plenty of women who'd made their interest clear, most of them with dollar signs over their eyes like cartoon characters.

But that wasn't Ainsley; she'd never been part of his circle of friends. Four years younger than him, they hadn't even been in high school together. And if she had liked him, she had too much self-respect to be overt about her feelings. So today, he'd flirted with her. At least he thought he had. She'd smiled. That was a good start. *Phase One: Win Ainsley's Attention.* As mad as he was at himself for getting into this without a solid plan, at least he hadn't completely screwed up.

Now I just need a Phase Two...

"SO, COOP," PHILIP STARTED, passing the mashed potatoes down the table to Kyle, "how was your day?" Claire had expected Kyle to stay as usual; dinner was his payment for picking up Cooper. Since he started his shifts at 7 PM, picking him up at 3:30 wasn't bad, and he did get a free meal out of it.

"Miss Buchanan's getting married."

Kyle stopped chewing his steak. "What did you say?"

"That's wonderful," Claire cooed, tossing her straight red hair. "Who's she marrying?"

Cooper shrugged, poking at the sautéed green beans on his plate.

Wonderful? thought Kyle. *That's the worst news I've ever heard. Also, is that little sneak trying to divert attention from Tree-Peeing Gate?*

"She didn't say?" Claire probed.

Cooper shook his head, and Kyle turned to his sister-in-law.

"You're the queen of Timber Falls gossip, why haven't I heard about this?"

"I hadn't heard a thing, but most of my gossip channels are hospital-related."

"Why the sudden interest?" His brother Philip smirked. "Is the most eligible bachelor in Timber Falls ready to settle down?" Kyle flipped him off by rubbing his eye with his middle finger and Philip returned the gesture.

"Quit it," Claire warned, getting up to retrieve her infant daughter from her bedroom down the hall. "He's six, not an idiot."

"Can I go play the tablet?" Cooper asked, and Philip nodded.

"Still haven't heard an answer," he added, directing a pointed look at Kyle, who'd given up eating all together.

"It's not sudden, and you know it."

"Seems like you missed your chance, bud."

Kyle worried his lower lip between his fingers. "You think?"

Philip shrugged. "That's what the six-year-old scuttlebutt would indicate."

"Who could she even be dating? Wouldn't we have heard something about it before now? Daniel hasn't said anything, he keeps tabs on her." Kyle got to his feet. Pacing would work, pacing would help. He could think better if he was moving. Better to panic moving than to panic sitting still.

"Friendship isn't exactly the same as keeping tabs, but okay." His brother pointed with his fork. "Internet. Could've met him on the internet, I hear that's the thing now."

"Okay, Grandpa."

Philip threw his arms out. "I'm practically a millennial!"

"No, you're not." He paused. "You don't think she's back with Dean, do you?"

"Dean moved to Portland."

"Dean belongs in Portland."

"Yes, Dean does belong in Portland. Weirdo."

"Remember when he dyed his hair black?"

"Weirdo."

"Who's a weirdo?" asked Claire, flopping back down at the table with Hannah in her arms.

"Dean Hoppsteader."

"Didn't he move to Portland?" Claire picked up her fork to resume eating, but Hannah couldn't stay latched. Her high-pitched cries tugged at Kyle's heartstrings, but he tried not to let it show. Infant cries were one of the few things that made him teary if he was already on edge.

He coughed, pivoting to give Claire some privacy as she tried to adjust her hold on Hannah. "We have lactation consultants at the hospital, you know."

Claire snorted. "I don't need a lactation consultant."

"I'm just saying. If you did, we have them."

His sister-in-law enunciated her words patronizingly. "I have done this before with Coop. I don't need a lactation consultant; they're the same breasts I had then."

"But not the same baby," her husband added gently, reaching over to rub her back.

"Don't touch," Claire said without looking up, still trying to get Hannah to latch, and Kyle felt momentary sympathy for his brother.

"I've got to get to work. Thanks for dinner, Claire."

"Thanks for picking up Cooper, Kyle. I should be able to do it myself soon, I've just been so exhausted, and Hannah's still nursing a lot..."

"Don't worry about it," he said, waving her off. "I don't mind." He paused at the threshold of the open front door. "Also, Ainsley caught him peeing on a tree at school. Bye." Kyle shut the door behind him before he could hear their reaction. He felt only slightly guilty for throwing Coop under the bus, since he had given him the idea. He whipped out his phone as he got in the car. Daniel. His brother would know, he'd been best friends with her since middle school.

Kyle: Is Ainsley engaged?

Daniel: Don't think so. Why?

Kyle: Heard a rumor.

Daniel: Pretty sure she would've told me or Winnie...

Kyle: Probably just a rumor.

Kyle: Don't tell her I said anything.

Daniel: But come to think of it, she has been on a few dates with some guy she met on an app, so I could be wrong.

So maybe it is true. That was upsetting for two reasons: she'd been dating someone, and she'd debased herself to use one of those terrible apps. Kyle wished he could say the same of the two of them. It felt like every time he came home and wanted to chill in his own living room, his brother and his brother's fiancée had beaten him to it. At least he was working nights now; the house was quieter during the day. Kyle liked quiet. Kyle missed quiet. He didn't regret letting Daniel move into his house, but he could be a little...

"A little much," Kyle grumbled aloud as he started his car.

———— ❧ ————

Pre-order *Must Be a Mistake* now!

—⁓❦⁓—

Can't wait? Need a little more Timber Falls **right now**? Newsletter subscribers get the exclusive short story, *How It All Began*, which tells us how Evan and Farrah met (that's Daniel and Kyle's mom and dad). Sign up now at https://www.sub-scribepage.com/timberfalls.

Acknowledgments

I SWEAR, THIS PART gets harder every time. The Tempest and Kite team is small, but boy, you ladies sure pour your hearts into this as much as I do, and that cannot go overlooked.

To my editorial team at Salt and Sage: you all rock. I can't say it enough: your professionalism, straight-up knowledge of your genres, and kindness make this so much easier.

To my critique partners, Angela Boord and Rebecca: you are both so good at picking out the little discontinuities, the little moments that could be amped up, pulling out what's good, but could be better. I'm so blessed that you enjoy reading my work.

To my sensitivity/expert readers, Erin and Jessica: thank you for helping me make this book medically accurate! I so appreciate your time and your insights.

To my copy editor, Jessica Gardner: Thank you for sharing your expertise with me! I'm still floored by all the rules you know. All those tiny corrections take my diamond in the rough and polish it up!

To my cover artist, Erin O'Neill-Jones: Wow. Just wow. I still can't get over how you've captured these characters! Thanks for all your hard work on this.

To my writing group, Ruth and Magalie: I will miss you so much. I will miss our talks over tea, your insights into the world, your companionable silences, your "we get it" reassurances. I carry the lessons I've learned from you into this new phase of my life, and I expect to see you over Zoom frequently, so don't think you're rid of me. That's not a thing. Love you, ladies.

To everyone who's helped promote the book: Meghan Lloyd, Heather Clark, Janna, Geornesna Clayton, and everyone who reviewed the book on NetGalley. Your support means so much to me! Truly, thank you.

Gratitude also to Matt McCarthy for his book *The Real Doctor Will See You Shortly* and Adam Kay for his book *This is Going to Hurt* for giving me a glimpse into the real lives of new doctors.

And last, but certainly not least, thank you to my CFO, Mr. West. I'm so thankful to have you as my sidekick. You may not wear a cape, babe, but you're my hero for so many reasons.

Connect with Fiona!

Thanks so much for taking the time to sample my work. I hope you enjoyed reading it even more than I enjoyed writing it, though I doubt that's possible. Being an author is a dream come true, and getting to share my books with delightful, thoughtful readers like you just adds to the sweetness. Drop me a line and let me know what you thought or leave a review on Goodreads!

Sign up for my bi-monthly newsletter, The West Wind, for freebies, deleted scenes, book reviews, and insight into my writing process at https://www.subscribepage.com/timber-falls.

On Twitter as @FionaWestAuthor
On Facebook as @authorfionawest
On Instagram as fionawestauthor
On Goodreads as Fiona West
Or email me at fiona@fionawest.net.
I love talking to fans!

CPSIA information can be obtained
at www.ICGtesting.com
Printed in the USA
LVHW092232081220
673640LV00034BA/345